CRAB'S HOLE

CRAB'S HOLE

A Family Story of Tangier Island

Anne Hughes Jander

THE LITERARY HOUSE PRESS • WASHINGTON COLLEGE
CHESTERTOWN, MARYLAND

The Literary House Press, Washington College
Chestertown, Md. 21620-1681
© 1994 by Owen Jander
All rights reserved. Published 1994; Second printing 1994
Printed in the United States of America
Cover: Illustrations taken from Jander family photographs, 1943-1952

Library of Congress Catalog Card Number: 94-78606

ISBN 0-937692-11-5

CONTENTS

FOREWORD

———

WHO HASN'T THOUGHT, at least briefly, of chucking it all and moving to an island? Islands have been called our original alternative societies. Their very boundedness, their insulation from the world, make one know something different must go on there.

Perhaps the attraction extends as deep as a symbolic re-entry of the womb, embraced fetus-like by the nurturing amniotic fluid. Or maybe it is the allure of a place small and defined enough that one can know, and be known, intimately; can even hope to make a difference.

Crab's Hole, Anne Hughes Jander's delightful memoir, is a rare and discerning look into the society of one of America's oldest and most durable island communities—Tangier, Virginia, a village of nearly a thousand souls, where descendants of the Crocketts and Pruitts and Thomases who settled the place more than three centuries ago still pursue the traditional life of Chesapeake Bay watermen.

The Janders, Anne and Henry, first went to Tangier as a lark, picking it from a map solely for its interesting isolation, more than ten miles from the nearest Chesapeake mainland. But they would end by abandoning a prosperous New England existence, moving kids, pets, and all to the remote marsh dab for nearly a decade.

Anne's comment on their decision, though it was made more than fifty years ago, strikes a chord that seems all too 1990s: "In [Connecticut] we were not truly living. The telephone began ringing in our house often at six in the morning—and continued 'til late at night, interrupting practically every meal... Henry's occupation as a builder had made him the property of architects and clients... our four children at one point attended four different schools... I had become a taxi driver... no time but for the most hurried chats with [friends]."

But it was the simple earnestness and openness of the Tangier Islanders that ultimately drew them. Anne writes movingly of being invited to the local church where they were announced to the whole congregation, which to a person, stopped to shake their hands as they filed out.

This scene, along with so many others she draws, rang strong and true with my wife and me. For three years in the 1980s we had moved our household to Smith Island, Tangier's neighbor six miles to the north in the Maryland Chesapeake. So often we would accompany guests to the little Methodist church there, and an islander would get up and say something about them, and how glad they were to have them visit. It sounds a small thing to write it, but this simple act of caring never failed to touch strangers deeply. It is perhaps a comment on some civility lacking in the rest of the world.

To me, a great pleasure of the Jander memoir lies in reading how a unique place has shaped a unique people. I believe this occurs everywhere to a degree; that, as Lawrence Durrell once wrote, if you were to wipe the French countryside clean of humans and begin over again, it would again give you Frenchmen, surely as it grows good wine grapes. On islands more than most places, these connections are stronger and more discernible.

Though they were anything but self-aggrandizing, the memoir is also very much about the Janders themselves. They were a remarkable family, taking in stride the bugs, bleak winters, high tides and rumors of "German spies." They could turn privation into great fun—outfitting "Bermuda," their outhouse, with picture windows, creating natural vistas such as seldom accompany bowel movements. They gave as good as they got, importing the first milk cows most islanders had ever seen; playing a key role in the electrification of the island in 1947.

They had, in fact, come to Tangier on the cusp of great change. The island they encountered in 1943 probably had changed less in the century preceding than it would by the time they departed in 1952.

You will enjoy the Janders' tales of the islanders' old ways, of speech patterns harking to Elizabethan England, of childhoods that seemed a cross of Huck Finn and Norman Rockwell; but be cautioned, you may well catch the urge to seek an island yourself.

Tom Horton

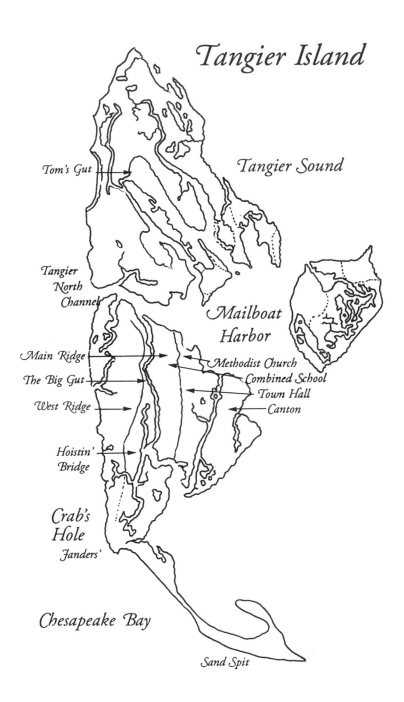

Tangier Island

Tangier Sound

Tom's Gut

Tangier
North
Channel

Mailboat
Harbor

Main Ridge
The Big Gut
West Ridge

Methodist Church
Combined School
Town Hall
Canton

Hoistin'
Bridge

Crab's
Hole

Janders'

Chesapeake Bay

Sand Spit

IN THE FOOTSTEPS
OF CAPTAIN JOHN SMITH

B ECAUSE OF AN ICE STORM we found Crab's Hole. In February
of 1943, early in the war, a sleety rain turned to ice and
clung heavily on the branches of trees throughout central
Virginia, at the same time spreading its shimmery danger along all
the roads leading out of Fredericksburg, where Henry and I were on
an early lap of a winter's holiday. We were traveling without a car,
because of the gas restrictions of those days, and had planned to
venture by bus to Charlottesville and thence back to colonial
Williamsburg. Since the ice storm forced us to abandon our goal of
visiting Jefferson's Monticello and the University of Virginia, we
made our way by delayed trains to Williamsburg, which we discovered had changed from the peaceful town we had once known, to a
horribly busy military camp center, in and out of which swarmed
the wives of hundreds and hundreds of Seabees and Navy officers.
Optimistic as usual, we had made no reservations, and so were
compelled to sit up all night in the lounge of the Williamsburg
Lodge, grateful as puppies to be let in from the cold.

We were certain that somewhere in this area there must be a
quiet spot the Army and Navy hadn't taken over, a place where

1

we could vacation for a few days. So we got out a map and studied it closely. What we eventually found was a small island, shaped like a fishhook, almost in the middle of the Chesapeake Bay: "Tangier Island."

"Let's find out what that island is like," proposed Henry—and I quickly seconded the idea. It was only with considerable determination that we were able to discover the complicated itinerary involved in reaching the place. By ferry, by bus, and by taxi we arrived at Crisfield, Maryland, from which small port, we had been told, one could take a mail boat out to Tangier Island. We reached Crisfield in the late afternoon, only to discover that the mail boat had already departed. By this time there was no turning back, of course. Our spirit of adventure had been aroused; and so we spent the night in a tourist home, and the next morning exploring the oyster-shucking and crab-picking houses down by the wharves. Crisfield, we learned, was the seafood capital of the Eastern Shore.

The genial captain of the Tangier mail boat not only agreed to our request to sit out on the deck for the two-hour ride across the Bay, but even joined us for much of the way, leaving his wheel to one of the passengers who were enjoying a much warmer crossing in the small cabin.

"Yes," he said to our questions, "quite a lot of folks come over here to see our island in the summertime—not many in the winter, though, once the ducking season's over."

We had been watching what was first just a speck on the horizon grow and grow until we could distinguish a tall church steeple, and finally many white houses set close together along what appeared to be one long street. Captain Thomas corrected us, however, and said that there were two long streets running parallel, the farther one hidden from the sight of boats entering the small harbor. Following a series of channel markers we neared the island. As the boat drew close to the wharf and we alighted, we were subjected to stares from a dozen or more youngsters of various ages who were there to meet the mail. Several men were on the dock with large two-wheeled pushcarts, and we loitered long enough to see the carts loaded with boxes of groceries for the village stores, bags of feed and coal, and the bags of U.S. mail and parcels post.

Captain Thomas, in response to our queries about lodging for the night, directed us to the home of Cap'n Josh and Miss Amanda Pruitt. "They're a nice couple, and they take in roomers. Anybody will show you where they live."

He was correct. As we walked down the very narrow street, lined on both sides with white houses, each one proudly displaying its small lawn neatly outlined with a whitewashed picket fence, we were ushered along by kindly villagers who finally pointed out a somewhat larger house to be that of Cap'n Josh. I think we should have known without their help, however, for seated in a chair on the lawn, behind the fence, was an old gentleman whose face we couldn't have forgotten had we never glimpsed it again. Enjoying the warm Virginia sunshine of a pleasant, late February day, he sat surrounded by billows of filmy white fishing net. In his hands was a hook which he used to attach the net to a stout rope. He was a man in his late seventies, we judged, with snow-white hair and a strong, firm face on which the years had left only a gentleness that was evident also in his voice as he assured us that indeed he was Cap'n Josh.

"Excuse my sitting down," he asked, "but it is hard for me to get up nowadays. If you'll just go right in my wife will take care of you."

At our knock came Miss Amanda, somewhat bent in figure, but with a youthful face and smile. The warm sun of outdoors wasn't present in the hall, but we followed our hostess to a cheerful up-stairs room where she lighted a small portable oilstove and invited us to be comfortable. We paid her in advance for the room—the amazing price of fifty cents apiece per night.

"We can't get fancy prices around here," she smiled, "for we don't have any modern conveniences."

By this time it was two-thirty, and Henry and I were completely famished after our trip across the water.

"I used to take boarders, too," Miss Amanda explained to us apologetically, "but the doctor has told me that I'd have to give that up. Perhaps Mrs. Rob Williams in the store up by the dock will make you a sandwich and a cup of coffee."

Retracing our steps we found Rob Williams's store, at the rear of which was a tiny room with a table and chairs. The storekeeper's wife apparently did not run a restaurant in the usual sense of the word, but she quickly managed to prepare us some hamburgers, and also promised to have some dinner for us at five-thirty.

In the afternoon we walked the length of the main street, past the four principal stores, the post office, and the small moving picture theater. Folk whom we stopped to question were willing to vouchsafe information, and we learned that the electricity on the island was produced by a small plant which couldn't give twenty-four-hour-service, but produced current only from five in the afternoon until ten-thirty at night. As we reached the end of the street—which, by this time we had been told, was called a "ridge"— we crossed over a long strip of marshland, broken by canals, one or two running longitudinally and others extending from these to the ridge we had just left and to the one we were approaching. The other ridge was less closely built up, with houses on just one side of the path. On this ridge, the "West Ridge," the path was of clay, rather than the strip of asphalt surface on the "Main Ridge." As we finally meandered again over the arched bridges that crossed the canals at the opposite end of the island and came once more to the white fences of the Main Ridge we were in time to see the lights suddenly twinkle forth up and down the island's length.

After eating a delicious fried chicken dinner with our new friends, the Rob Williamses, we sat around the store where a number of men were assembled. Listening to their conversation we became aware that they were talking about the oyster catch of the day and about the success of the Tangiermen who were crab-dredging down the bay. Gradually Henry and I were included in the talk until finally we realized that it was we who were doing the talking, and the men the listening.

By now we had ascertained that Cap'n Eulice, the mail boat captain, lived on the West Ridge; and so we decided to risk the darkness of the marsh path to visit him. Our knock on the door was answered by a pretty woman with beautiful, wavy hair, who greeted us with a friendly, twinkling smile.

"Is this the home of Cap'n Eulice Thomas of the mail boat?" we inquired.

"It is that, but he's gone over." ("Gone over" is the Tangier way of saying "gone over to the other ridge.") "He'll be back directly, though. Won't you come in?"

"You are Mrs. Thomas, I guess?" She nodded yes. "We met your husband on the boat today and enjoyed talking with him so much we thought we'd like to become better acquainted."

"Well, do come in and wait for him. He'll be sorry if he misses you." We followed her into a large comfortable room heated by a small oil burner. When we were seated, our hostess resumed the handwork she had left to answer our knock.

"What a beautiful rug," I exclaimed in admiration; and Mrs. Thomas, pleased, spread out her work that I might see the pattern she was crocheting.

"Do you do handwork yourself?" she asked. I admitted to a very small knowledge of crocheting and an even smaller one of knitting. Henry temporarily forgotten, we launched into a discussion of fancywork, thence continuing to cooking and to the exchange of recipes—all of which kept us entertained until the door opened to admit Cap'n Eulice.

"Well, I see you have company, Hattie," he exclaimed. "I'd hoped I might run into you folks over on the Main Ridge," he continued. "I didn't have an idea that you'd be over here."

"Glad to see you, Cap'n Eulice," piped up Henry. "These women have talked crocheting and the mysteries of baking German fruitbread ever since we got in here!"

"Can't we have something to eat, Hattie?" asked Eulice; but already Hattie was on her way to the kitchen. Within a few minutes we were sitting around the kitchen table drinking coffee, and enjoying our introduction to a favorite Tangier dessert: sweet potato pie. We ate a great deal. And we talked and talked—until suddenly we realized that the lights would be turned off at ten-thirty; so with haste we said a grateful good-night, and started back for the haven of Cap'n Josh's home. Just as we reached the comparative safety of the Main Ridge, in fact, the lights went out, leaving us shivering at the thought of crossing that marsh in the darkness, and stumbling off that narrow path into the chilly waters of the canal.

Cap'n Josh and Miss Amanda were sitting up, waiting for us with an extra little kerosene lamp for us to take upstairs. For an hour or more yet we sat with that sweet couple, listening to tales of fishing as it used to be on Chesapeake Bay and to the early history of Tangier. We went to sleep between soft flannel blankets instead of sheets. Warm and cozy though we were, it was a long time before I fell off to sleep. I kept thinking of John Crockett and his wife who had come here back in 1686 with their family of eight sons and daughters, whose descendants now number almost a third of Tangier's inhabitants. And my mind pictured the figure of Parson Thomas, the distant ancestor of Cap'n Eulice, whose thunderous sermon of warning to the British encamped on Tangier in 1812 had, according to Cap'n Josh, proved a true prophecy of their failure to take the city of Baltimore. Only gradually did I fall asleep.

The big event of the day on the island, we discovered, was the arrival of the mail boat. Next afternoon we joined the group of eager children on the wharf to greet the returning people who had been over to Crisfield to do special shopping. As we walked back toward the village we chanced to enter into conversation with a pleasant, open-faced woman of perhaps forty-five years, who had returned from visiting her son, a schoolteacher in Crisfield.

"Have you been here long?" she asked, as we walked across the dock with her.

"We came just yesterday, in fact; but we like it so much that we've decided to stay a day or two longer," we answered. "Do you mind if we walk along the road with you; we have nothing special to do this afternoon?"

"Indeed I don't. I like to talk to strangers who come on here. Have you been to the beach yet?"

"No, we've wondered about that...whether you could get to it without a boat."

"If you'll walk as far as my house, it's just a little farther on to the bayside; and I'll take you over there if you'd like."

We assented eagerly. Again crossing the marsh on the path we had followed the previous day, this time we continued down a side lane past half-a-dozen houses or more, and then along a raised diking, built, our new friend told us, by the British many years ago, over a strip of rather muddy marshland. Suddenly the beach was before us. In both directions it stretched as far as could be seen. Accustomed as Henry and I were to the rocky shores of Connecticut's beaches on Long Island Sound, we were delighted by all that sand; and we walked some distance along the shore. Looking back toward the island's houses we noticed a rather dilapidated house at the southern end of the West Ridge, separated from the rest of the ridge by a stretch of vacant land.

When we drew attention to the charming location of this house, Mrs. Crockett remarked, "That's a place you could buy if you wanted to. It's too far from the dock, so nobody wants to live way down there."

Already the spirit of Tangier had struck into my heart. As Henry and I exchanged a somewhat meaningful glance, I sensed that the same spirit had also gripped him. Impetuously I exclaimed, "Couldn't we buy it—just as a little place to visit in the summer sometimes?"

"I wish you would buy it," our guide said with obvious sincerity. "I should love to have you for neighbors."

We were back once more to the road, and Mrs. Crockett paused at one of the houses bordering it.

"This is where I live. Won't you come in for a minute?" she said simply. We accepted, for we were drawn to this natural, genuine woman as we had been to Hattie and Eulice Thomas, and to Cap'n Josh and Miss Amanda. Mrs. Crockett's house was very chilly at first, but in the center of the sitting room was a small iron stove into which our hostess piled paper and wood, pouring over it kerosene with such efficiency that within a couple of minutes she had created a fire so intense that we found ourselves pushing our rocking chairs back from its heat. As we sat waiting for the kettle to boil, Mrs. Crockett told us of her other son who had gone from the island to the University of Virginia. After his graduation he had then been chosen for the Navy's v-12 program. Justifiable pride was apparent in her face as she showed us the pictures of her two fine looking sons.

"We had a hard struggle educating them," she confided. "Crabs and oysters weren't bringing the prices a few years ago that they fetch now, and so we had to scrimp a lot. I went out and did wall-papering for people, to help out. We managed somehow—and it sure was worth it!"

As she talked she was setting a table in the kitchen adjoining. She served us coffee and homemade rolls, and, along with that, fig preserves—and so we were treated to another Tangier specialty. We had noticed a great many shrub-like trees, unknown to us, growing on the island, and we now learned that these were fig trees. It seemed to us that nothing could excel Mrs. Crockett's fig preserves. Imagine our delight when she wrapped up a quart jar of her preserves for us to take home to our children.

As we took our departure Mrs. Crockett said shyly, "If you really would like to have that house I'll enquire and see what you can get it for."

Without looking to Henry for acquiescence I said, "Please do." Walking across the marsh toward the store and supper, I remarked to Henry, rather timidly, "Now I suppose I've gone and done it." To my surprise he answered, very quietly, "Well, it would be nice to be able to come here often."

A certain "Tangier something" that had affected me had obviously affected my husband, as well.

Cap'n Josh had invited us to attend prayer meeting that night. Instead of being held in the big white church it was conducted—in an effort to conserve fuel—in the small hall belonging to the lodge of The Daughters of America. Perhaps seventy-five people were there to hear their minister explain passages of scripture and to spend a few moments in prayer. The hymns were sung with great gusto, somewhat slowly and with considerable freedom of style, but with much joy and fervor. The meeting was about to be disbanded when Cap'n Josh stood up to speak. "Friends," he said quietly, "we have with us tonight a couple from off the island who seem to like our town very much, and I would like you all to meet them. Before you go will you all stop to shake hands with Mr. Jander and Mrs. Jander?"

As they left the hall one and all came to us and shook our hands so earnestly that again our hearts were touched. I didn't dare look toward Henry lest he notice the shine of tears in my eyes.

Next day on the boat returning to Crisfield Cap'n Eulice explained it all to us.

"Did you get your feet muddy yesterday when you walked on the beach? If you did it's all up with you! They say that once you get the mud of Tangier Island between your toes you can never stay away from the place long."

So that was the answer. It wasn't the extraordinary spirit of its friendly people—or any other mysterious "Tangier something"—it was just the mud of the island between our toes.

ACQUISITION
AND CHRISTENING

T HE LITTLE HOUSE ON THE SOUTHWEST END of the island proved to be difficult to obtain—a sore trial to my impatient nature.

Having fallen in love with Tangier, I was in a constant dither lest someone else get the house before we did. Four years later such fears might have been well founded, for even on isolated Tangier Island property was to feel the post-war housing shortage. At that time, however, there were no returning veterans and their brides to consider. The little house we wanted was separated from the other houses on the ridge by a good five hundred yards; and Tangier women prefer to be close to their neighbors. Furthermore, the house was located about a mile from the main docks. Tangier watermen, we learned, understandably like to be near their boats. They arise early in the morning, sometimes in the blackness of night if the tides demand it, to go to their crabbing fields and oyster grounds. A long walk to the dock is nothing they relish. To make our chosen house still more unpopular, it had been owned previously, we found, by a very energetic man who, in addition to tilling the few acres that surround the house, had made and sold coffins. The little building in which the coffins had been stored was still there—and was supposed to be haunted. (We have looked in vain for some sign of our ghost to thank him for his assistance in the purchase of our Tangier home; but except for a howl in the roof gutter during a northwester, there has been no trace of him.)

We had visited the island first in the month of February, but it wasn't until the following October that we discovered definitely who owned that house. In the meantime we had brought our youngest son, Mark, then nine, to spend a few weeks in the home of Eulice and Hattie Thomas, and their young son, Rudy. Hattie and Rudy then came up with Mark to visit us in Connecticut that summer. In the interim Lenore Crockett, our hostess at coffee on our first visit, had turned seriously ill, and was unable to help us. Finally, a letter came from Hattie in October informing us that some people from Baltimore had expressed interest in the property. The next afternoon found me on Tangier Island, having dropped everything to save "my house"—as I now thought of it—from the grasp of the Baltimoreans. The actual owner of the house, it had been determined, was Captain Peter Williams, an active businessman of the village; and so, accompanied by Hattie, I paid a call on Cap'n Pete that very evening. He was a small, energetic, and pleasant old man, with a most kindly wife whom Hattie called Miss Rose.

"This is Mrs. Jander from Connecticut," Hattie introduced me. "She's interested in Severn Crockett's house, and I told her you own it now."

"Sit down, sit down," said Cap'n Pete, as he drew chairs up for us. "What do you want of a house way down there at the end of the West Ridge? Wouldn't you prefer one up this way farther?"

"No, Cap'n Pete," I said, forgetting all the rules of bargaining. "I've fallen in love with that particular spot, and I've persuaded my husband to buy it, if you'll sell, and if the price is reasonable." I was breathless in my eagerness.

"The trouble is, I've sort of half promised to sell that house to someone else. I don't know their names, but they're friends of the family my granddaughter is going to marry into." He turned to Hattie. "Friends of Lenore Crockett, Hattie."

"Why, she's the one who first told us the house was for sale, Cap'n Pete!," I interrupted hastily. "She took us to the beach one day last winter and pointed out the old house to us and said she thought it was for sale. She promised me she'd find out whether it could be bought." I turned to Hattie for confirmation of my story.

"Yes, that's right, Cap'n Pete," affirmed Hattie. "Lenore's been writing to them ever since last winter."

"Well, now that's different," said the old gentleman. "I wouldn't be able to say right now whether or not I would sell it, but I tell you what I'll do. I'll think it over."

"I have to leave in a day or so, Cap'n Pete," I urged. "Couldn't I come to see you tomorrow evening about it?"

"Come by, anyhow. Rose and I are always glad to have folks visit us."

We were about to leave when Miss Rose urged us to stay to have a piece of her fruit cake which she had made early that year. Before I began to eat the cake I determined to praise it highly, whether I liked it or not, hoping to make a good impression on Cap'n Pete and his wife. But one bite dispersed my deceitful intentions. It was without doubt the most delicious fruitcake I had ever eaten, and to my pleasure Miss Rose confided her secret in making it—little chips of gum drops were sprinkled all through the batter before baking. I found out from Hattie on the homeward way that Miss Rose was considered one of the best cooks on Tangier; and I fully agreed.

That night I laughed to myself in bed at the picture I had drawn in my mind of the horrible Baltimorean competitors for the house on the point.

Next evening found Hattie and me again at Cap'n Pete's home. After preliminary small talk Cap'n Pete motioned me to follow him. We walked through several immaculate rooms to the front parlor, in the beautiful tidiness of which we were to discuss the purchase of the house. On the mantel were several photographs. These Cap'n Pete showed me with pride.

"This is my son who is Commissioner of the docks in Boston," he said, as I viewed the picture of an intelligent appearing young man with a strong resemblance to his mother,

"And this," went on my host, "is the son I lost. "It's his daughter who's going to marry Lenore's son." Tears came to the old man's voice.

"This one," I said, "must be your granddaughter."

"Yes," he spoke proudly. "She is the one who's going to marry Willie. Such a fine boy he is, too. Been all through college, and now he's learning to be a dentist for the Navy."

"Yes, I remember his face," I told Cap'n Pete. "Lenore showed me his picture the day we met her last winter—the same day she showed me the old house."

"Well, now talking of the house, I've decided that if you really want that house you can have it. It's not much use to me; and my foster daughter who's been living there wants to move somewhere closer to the dock." Whereupon he quoted a price that was well above what Henry had given as the limit we should pay.

"But Cap'n Pete," I exclaimed, "that old house will need a great deal of repairing before it can be made comfortable. It leaks, and the walls are in bad shape. It hasn't any conveniences; and it's way down on the southern point, where nobody wants to live."

"I don't think I can sell it for any less," the Captain insisted. "It isn't very much, really, when you consider the price of houses on the mainland."

"I know that," I agreed, "but should we ever choose to sell it, we would have to consider the prices that houses bring on the island, and not what they bring elsewhere." (My experience as a house-builder's wife was coming to the fore.) "Are you sure that's the best price you can offer? I just know that my husband won't agree to paying that much."

"I'm afraid that's the best I can do."

Knowing that even my persuasion, and Henry's growing fondness for Tangier would not be sufficient to induce my husband to spend so much for what, at that point, seemed to be merely a vacation cottage, my spirits dropped. My eyes filled with tears.

"I guess I'd better go, then, Cap'n Pete, before I start crying and make a fool of myself." Gulping, I hastened before him, back to the sitting room, where Hattie and Miss Rose gazed, startled, at my reddened face. Feeling about as silly as I could, I rushed Hattie out with me to the cover of darkness where I could cry in comfort.

The following morning I said a discouraged farewell to Hattie, and walked with Eulice to the mailboat. There we were met by Cap'n Pete, who drew me aside.

"My wife says I should let you have that house for what you feel it's worth. I didn't have any idea you wanted it so badly; but Rose thinks maybe you and your husband will be a help to the island if you come down here to live. So when you come with your husband next time, tell him to come to see me. I'll not sell the house 'til he comes." I could have hugged the old gentleman—and very nearly did.

All the way back to Connecticut on the train Cap'n Pete's words echoed in my mind: "…if you come here to live." "To live" had never entered our minds. We had pictured ourselves going occasionally to the island for a rest from the everlasting race of life which is the commuter's lot. But, "to live on the island…to live there?"

Within me I knew that, in Westport, we were not truly living. The telephone began ringing in our house often at six in the morning—and continued 'til late at night, interrupting practically every meal. Henry's occupation as a builder had made him the property of architects and clients. Even his Sundays were no longer his. We had both become involved in clubs, churchwork, and choirs. Our four children at one point attended four different schools, which necessitated membership in four separate Parent-Teachers' Associations. I made sandwiches for teas, sold tickets for benefits, and served on hordes of committees. Our evenings, if there weren't some community or church meeting to attend, were consumed in a constant round of parties and obligatory entertaining. We had many and good friends, but rarely had time to have any but the most hurried chats with them. The children went to music lessons, to dancing school, to Girl Scouts and to Boy Scouts. And because, in Westport, we lived a mile from the center of town I had become a taxi driver for a large part of every day.

Live? This was not what I believed life should be at its best; yet here was time fast slipping away—the years with our children growing fewer, and middle age creeping upon us.

By the time the train had pulled into Pennsylvania Station all was settled: we were going to pull up roots and move to Tangier. At that moment there remained but the necessity of persuading Henry—which, from experience, I sensed might be easily accomplished.

And so it was. Henry had suffered more than I under the stress of long and tiresome duties. Move to Tangier? With only the briefest hesitation he embraced the vision.

His business partner, our relatives, and our friends were aghast at our announcement. "Why don't you just pull out of so many activities if they're wearying you?" was the usual question. Patiently we tried to explain that to survive in an expensive metropolitan area required ceaseless activity for a builder to be able to meet competition and to make ends meet. Too, we pointed out that we seemed to be the kind of folk who just manage to get involved—who couldn't say "no" to a desperate committee chairman, or a harassed minister, or a friend who was getting up a party. (We've noticed that the very friends who, at that point, urged that we cut back on our social and business activities have not been able to do the same themselves —and they write us regularly about being "up to their necks.")

"But you don't have enough money to "retire," pointed out one of our most beloved friends—who was also our lawyer. (Having made out our income tax returns for many years, Max was in a position to submit that judgment.)

"There'll be enough to help with the children's education. We can count on them to do their share. On the island the whole family will just have to live less expensively. Henry can do enough building work in the village to keep the wolf from the door. We'll have a garden, and have some pigs and chickens. We'll survive. At the end we can always go to the poorhouse!" Thus ran our argument.

At last, with pitying glances toward Henry—whom all believed to be the victim of a slightly cracked wife—they gave up their efforts at dissuasion.

Thus, with not much money, with a lot of faith, much anticipation, sorrow at leaving many dear friends, and fortunately with at least the semi-approval of our four youngsters, we proceeded with the purchase of the house and with moving plans. From that day on, by all who knew us in our Connecticut existence, we've been pronounced those "Crazy Janders."

Henry and Cap'n Pete hit it off well on our next trip and came to an agreement over the price of our new home—which, we decided, should be named "Crab's Hole." One day during that visit, as Henry and I were standing on one of the arched bridges along the marsh road, we gazed down toward the house in the distance and groped in our minds for a fitting name. Having discarded each idea that came to us, we thought simply to postpone the decision. As we walked along the diked path, however, we were watching with amusement the antics of the countless little fiddler crabs as, sensing our approach, they dashed for their holes in the clay bank. "I have it!" I shouted: "Crab's Hole." Henry approved and the name stuck.

"Crab's Hole" was a name that was to prove very right for our new home on Tangier Island. The whole family took to it. A year or so later, on one occasion when the family was seated at the supper table after a meal, we got to playing games with crab names, applying them to one another. Son Owen, who played the violin, was the family's obvious "fiddler crab." Mark, the youngest of our four children, had the lightest skin pigment, and was always the first to get sunburned—and blister, and peel—so he was appointed our "peeler crab."

Daughter Sylvia—as an adolescent inclined to plumpness—was dubbed our "soft-shell crab"; while her oldest brother, Kent—who was then serving in the Army—was the Jander "hard-shell crab."

And Henry? The family's "king crab," to be sure.

By this time Mark had learned how to get around in a boat and catch crabs, and so was our resident expert on such matters. In the vocabulary of the Chesapeake Bay watermen a female crab is a "sook;" and so I, logically, became the family sook.

(It's a conversation we have enjoyed recounting for our off-island guests!)

During the winter and spring Henry made a couple of prolonged stays on the island to work on the house and make it more livable. He took with him a couple of carpenters and a stonemason, as well as a considerable amount of building material, left from various construction jobs, which he had been patiently hoarding in our full-to-bursting barn in Connecticut. He couldn't resist remarking to me, "I told you so."

Whereas I am by instinct a thrower-outer, Henry has always been the opposite: a collector. "You see, dear," he said slyly, "I just knew that all this would come in handy some day"—and he was obviously right this time.

Under the friendly observation of numerous Tangier neighbors Crab's Hole acquired some new dormer windows and an array of built-in kitchen cabinets. Better yet, a handsome fireplace was constructed in the living room, with bookcases on both sides. Best of all, a couple of large bay windows were created for the kitchen and for the living room, affording us spacious views across the marshes at the southern end of the island, where there were no houses, and all was Nature. With these major operations out of the way Henry felt that it would be possible for the family to move into the house at the end of the school year.

In the building trades around New York City there are skilled workmen from the most diverse national backgrounds. Our building crew was no exception; and so the men who accompanied Henry included a Swede (Carl), an Italian (Giovanni, or just "John"), and another fellow who was second generation Bronx (Pete). Hattie Thomas was kind enough to board the three men during their stay on the island; and after suppertime they followed the custom of all good Tangiermen, and went up to sit for a time in one or another of the general stores. To be sure, they were fascinated by the Tangier accent, with its unique mixture of Elizabethan English, of Southern drawl, and idioms used by all watermen in the Chesapeake Bay area. (The musical sound of the human voice as it is heard on Tangier Island is like nothing else in the English-speaking world.) The townspeople of Tangier, on the other hand, were equally intrigued by the Scandinavian lilt in Carl's speech, and the Bronx twang in Pete's voice. John's Neapolitan accent they found almost unintelligible. Like most Neapolitans he was quite short; yet he was strong as an ox. His hair was gray, and he wore a small mustache. His face was round and cherubic, unwrinkled and rosy; and when he burst into his own jolly yet gentle smile, none could resist. The Tangier people accepted John Osimanti as a quite adorable friend.

John's moustache brings me to the subject of beards. Always I have coaxed Henry to wear one. It has always been my private opinion that every man should wear a moustache or a beard of one variety or another. Nature provides them with such a fine way by which, with the use of a little art and a little imagination, they can make themselves individually outstanding. There are as many sorts of beards and moustachios as there are ways of dressing a woman's hair; yet what do men do but, by shaving, imitate the smooth cheeks of the female of the species. Coaxing my husband to grow a beard, however, had always been in vain; in the New York City business world it wasn't done. However, as a joke, Henry decided to let his beard grow during a month's stay on the island during the remodeling of Crab's Hole. When he took his departure, one little girl ran back to her mother and reported that "that man who doesn't shave has gone home."

It was dark when I met the train that brought Henry home, and when suddenly I found myself being grabbed—and with fervor—by a rough-bearded man I was shocked and stunned. As I took a second look, however, I burst into laughter!

"Darling, you have a beard at last!"

"Not so nice as you thought it would be, eh?"

"Oh, I think it's wonderful! You mustn't shave it off."

"You don't think I'm going to the office with all this on my face, do you? I've just grown it for a joke." Worry was showing through the beard on his face.

"Tomorrow is Sunday. Surely you can leave it on for the weekend. Everybody will be so amused to see you in church. Leave it on for tomorrow, at least, just to give everyone a laugh."

The first step was accomplished. The beard went to church. Everyone did laugh, of course. But that night Henry prepared to shave. Fortunately, I discovered his intention before any damage had been done.

"Surely you aren't going to shave it off before you have it trimmed up in a nice little Van Dyke, just to see what it will look like," I begged.

"Good heavens, what will you be wanting me to do next?" he exclaimed. I think it was partly my persuasion, but partly his own curiosity to see what a Van Dyke would do for him, that resulted in his promise to leave the beard on until he could get to a barber. The result delighted me—and pleased him as well, obviously, for he wears his Van Dyke beard to this day.

Opinions are divided as to its beauty: there never seems to be any middle point of view. Either people think it is horrible, that it makes him look old (the opinion of most of his relatives), or else they think it is distinguished and makes him handsome. It really doesn't matter, anyhow, since I am the one who must get kissed, and I like a beard. Strange to say, the beard has been a definite asset in calling the attention of outsiders to the needs of our island town. Whenever Henry makes a call on some important official he is duly remembered because of his facial ornamentation. It was amusing, too, that when people learned of our moving to a remote island, they frequently asked whether the beard was required by the religious beliefs of the islanders. On the other hand, we learned after living a short time at Crab's Hole, that some of the Tangier people assumed that we came from a place in the world where all men wore beards. Such speculations to be caused merely by the growth of a few hairs on the masculine lip and chin!

FROM CONNECTICUT TO
THE CHESAPEAKE

————

MY CHILDHOOD DAYS were spent either in moving, getting ready to move, or in getting settled after the move, for my father was a minister who as a result of his own convictions chose not to serve a single congregation for more than a half-dozen years. There were no moving vans in those days and the furniture was always sent by freight, the cheapest way, since Father's salary was microscopic. For days before our belongings were removed from the parsonage we were leaving, we children wound newspapers around the legs of the furniture while listening to our parents discussing rather heatedly whether this article or that could withstand another journey. Mother was a hoarder and Father a thrower-outer. The situation being reversed in my own marriage—to make me the one anxious to be rid of unnecessary possessions—I managed, as moving day drew nigh, to empty our cellar, attic, and closets of a considerable amount of trash under the guise of patriotism, since those were the days of paper and metal drives. The barn, however, was sacred territory and the odds and ends of lumber, the millions of screws, bolts, nails, and bits of miscellaneous hardware therein were taken, as heretofore related, to

Tangier. Out of fairness to Henry it is my duty to report that, as a result of wartime shortages, almost every one of those countless screws, bolts, nails, etc., has been put to good use.

Our oldest son, Kent, chanced to be home on furlough from the Army and when the actual date of departure arrived, he and Henry went on ahead with the jalopy to arrange for the transport of the furniture from Crisfield to Tangier. It was left to me to supervise the emptying of the house and to follow the moving van with the remaining three children, the dog, the two cats, and our old Buick. Although we had decided definitely against taking Buttercup and Daisy (the cows), Maedchen, our German shepherd, and Cleo and Margaret, the cats, simply had to accompany us. Maedchen at the time was troubled with fleas which time didn't permit us to annihilate before we left. (The fleas didn't trouble us on the journey, but a couple of weeks later when we picked up the car at Crisfield to take a short trip on the peninsula we found it literally alive with descendants of the Connecticut insects which Maedchen had left behind on the car's upholstery.) Cleo, the mother cat, disapproved of the whole procedure of moving most vociferously. She was expecting again—she has to the moment produced thirty-two kittens and is again expecting—and was uneasy. Margaret, her young son, mistakenly named thus in honor of the daughter of our Westport minister whose birthday coincided with that of the kitten, was much happier and did much purring on the long ride to Virginia. We spent the night in two cabins. It was dusk when we drove in to the cabin grounds, so we didn't bother to mention the dog and the two cats to the proprietors. Maedchen slept under the bed of the two boys, and Cleo and Margaret spent the night with Sylvia and me. (I never pass those cabins on the way to New York but I wonder whether they harbored our fleas.)

Next morning we lost considerable time because of Cleo's unhappy state of mind. We drove into a side road to find a pleasant, private spot where the animals might wander about for a few minutes—whereupon Cleo promptly leapt toward the nearby woods. It took rapid chasing on the part of the children, assisted by

Maedchen, to waylay her. Poor cat, she didn't regain her composure for several weeks, not in fact until the birth of her new litter, whose foreign blood made them most interesting to Tangier children. (Instead of having to drown most of the kittens, as I usually found to be necessary, I managed to find homes for all of the little yellow fuzzballs.)

It would be an understatement to say that I was grateful to arrive at Crisfield. There were Henry and Kent, who had managed to hire a boat for the furniture. It really wasn't hired, however. Young Charlie Pruitt, a friendly and handsome Tangierman who had married a schoolteacher from off the island, needed a new roof for his house and had made a deal to provide his boat in return for the assistance of Henry and Owen in the work on his roof, which turned out to be a satisfactory arrangement all around. Charlie's boat is a good sized one and steady. Mark, unable to wait to see Tangier again, took Maedchen and left with the mail boat: but with the help of Charlie, the two moving men, and the other three children, we were soon able to transfer the "goods," as my father used to call our belongings, to the boat. Fortunately the day was calm and nothing was even dampened on the ride across Tangier Sound to our new home; but by the time we arrived at the island's dock, the tide was out and it was impossible for the second boat which was to carry the furniture down the canals to Crab's Hole to make the trip. There was no alternative but to leave everything on Charlie's big boat for the night, and with no beds at the house, to find for ourselves a resting place for our weary bones. Again Hattie came to our rescue, and with her generous hospitality managed to find room for us once more.

Tides were high next morning, so at dawn Henry and the boys were unloading from Charlie's boat to Willie Parks's smaller crabboat. Willie's boat could continue beyond the Big Gut through the smaller canal running parallel with the southern end of the West Ridge. There it, too, could go no farther; and so for the last hundred yards of the voyage everything was once more transferred to the small skiff belonging to Parker Thomas, whose services we had previously engaged for clearing the water bushes from our land. There was no lack of help. Every small boy and girl on the island, it seemed, was present; and no sooner did a new load arrive at Crab's Hole landing than dozens of small but willing hands were there to carry things on the last lap to the house. There was no use giving in to the fears that assailed us.

"Sylvia," I whispered apprehensively, "go tell Daddy to be careful to whom he hands those cartons. I've packed dishes in them, and these small youngsters will surely drop some of them."

Soon Sylvia returned to report, "Dad says this is no time to discriminate. You'll just have to pray!"

I determined to be philosophical. "Well, I suppose they can't do more harm to things than you four Jander offspring have already accomplished."

And strangely enough when the results were surveyed as the last small chair was brought from the skiff it was apparent that less damage had been done in the five handlings to which our possessions had been subjected than had previously been suffered in the process of moving from one house to another in the same town.

Our small grand piano caused a sensation—it was the first of its kind ever to appear on the island. The fact that its legs could be removed was astounding to the onlooking children. When the men had finally reassembled the little instrument there was immediate demand for music. There in our small living room, strewn now with boxes and barrels, we held the strangest concert in which we had ever participated. Owen at the violin; Henry, Sylvia, and Mark singing; with me accompanying them with hands still black with the grit of moving tasks. We could have had no more appreciative audience than the kindly watermen who were to be our neighbors, and the curious children who crowded about us.

Having deposited his family and furniture at Crab's Hole, Henry left for New York the next day. There were innumerable odds and ends to be finished up in the dissolving of a business partnership of more than twenty years' standing; and with four children to assist me, it was assumed that the task of settling shouldn't be too difficult. We had blithely entered on a life of relative pioneering, and now the test was upon me. For water there was only a small rain-water cistern, the contents of which would soon be exhausted. An empty cistern meant carrying all our water from the pump at Miss Sadie's, about two hundred yards up the West Ridge. Though there was a sink installed in its proper place in the kitchen, it as yet had no running water. We had managed to find some kerosene lamps and already owned several candlesticks, but quickly discovered that there was no use in lighting them to enable us to work at night since there were as yet no screens on our windows and doors. Even the tiny glow of a candle brought a zestful swarm of mosquitoes to feed upon our foreign flesh. This same lack of screens had already invited millions of flies into our house. The neighbors assured me that the mosquitoes were quite bad because of a recent rainy period; but since no special mention was made of the flies, I assumed that they were just the regular occurrence. To help things along, real summer weather came early that year. We had no icebox, and milk which was carried the long mile from Homer Williams's store had to be drunk almost instantly to keep it from going sour. Butter swam in the butterdish. We were hot and thirsty by the afternoon of our first day's attempt to bring order into our new home, and we were without ice even to cool the lukewarm water.

All day long children came to watch the progress we were making with the house. They came not individually, nor yet in groups of two or three, but in gangs of fifteen or twenty. We were all so anxious to be welcome in the community and to be found friendly that we went out of our way to be entertaining to our ever-increasing guests. We played the piano and violin, exhibiting the various rooms of the house and explained who would sleep where, and chatted as pleasantly as our tired backs, mosquito-chewed arms and legs, and thirsty tongues would allow. Sometimes there would come a lull. As the children sat with me in the bay window of the dining alcove, we could glance back through the kitchen window at the winding path crossing our land from our neighbor's property.

"Another contingent is approaching," Owen would announce —and groans would go forth from us all.

At dusk on the second night I practically crawled upstairs to bed. For the first time I allowed myself to wonder, "Has this just been one horrible mistake? Can I endure the flies and the mosquitoes, the children, and the inconveniences one more day?" A strong southwest wind was blowing, and the surf on the bay was so noisy that it seemed to be beating against the very windows of my bedroom. The sound of the wind and the water merely lulls me happily to sleep nowadays, but that night it added only dreariness to my heart as I stifled my sobs from the ears of my children, whose unhappiness I feared might be as great as my own.

Next day I awoke with the old Welsh stubbornness again to the fore. Leaving Sylvia to manage the last ends of unpacking, with the aid of her brothers, I caught the mail boat for Crisfield. There I sought the town's secondhand shop and made a purchase which was destined to bring us more comfort than anything I had ever bought in my entire life: an ancient, green, enamelled icebox which I straightaway arranged to have delivered at the wharf. Next I invested in a big handspray and a gallon of insect killer (the days of DDT, beloved DDT, had not yet come). Owen and Parker Thomas in the skiff were at the Tangier dock to meet me.

"Did you get it, Mom?" Owen shouted across from the dock as the mailboat drew near. I nodded assent.

"Thank goodness!" he shouted back. Turning to Parker, he said, "Tonight we'll have iced tea for supper!"

Together they hauled the green icebox into the skiff, and then placed alongside it a wonderful hundred-pound block of ice, carefully and lovingly covering it with a piece of canvas to retain as much as possible of its weight as Parker poled through Reuben's River, the Big Gut, and our own canal to Crab's Hole. That night we had our fill of gloriously cold iced tea and lemonade, and the next morning the milk was sweet and fresh, and the butter could be spread instead of poured onto our toast.

Miracles were beginning to happen. Next afternoon there

arrived on the boat the window screens that Henry had obtained for the house. Kent and Owen, having been provided with careful instructions from their father, managed by nightfall to install at least one screen per room. With the new spray every inch and corner of Crab's Hole had been cleared, temporarily at least, of mosquitoes, and all the flies had been swatted. That evening we were able to light our kerosene lamps, and all of us gathered around the family's dining room table to read by that soft light in peace.

Each day saw the hordes of visiting children diminish. After all, we had been inspected and found to be not much different from other people. Everyone had heard "the dish of music"—as one young neighbor called our Welsh jug with its built-in music box. Within a week or two our callers had subsided to a normal number, whose visits were truly welcome and enjoyable. And then, happiest miracle of all, Parker Thomas consented to come to work for us!

PARKER THOMAS

P ARKER THOMAS was a cousin of Cap'n Eulice, our mail
boat owner. Parker's father and Eulice's father had each
in his turn run the mail to the island from the mainland,
as had their fathers before them. The Thomases traced their ances-
try back to Joshua Thomas, who gained considerable local fame for
his fearless Christian character, and for having carried the creed
of Methodism to the islands of the Chesapeake. This was the
same staunch figure who had prophesied the failure of the British at
Baltimore.

It was friend Eulice who recommended Parker to Henry as a
man who could help us to clear all that land that went with Crab's
Hole, and who could keep watch over the place until we arrived
there.

Parker performed these simple jobs so conscientiously that, although we had never entertained the idea of employing any help at
Crab's Hole, Parker became not just useful, but precious. And so, in
a quite informal sense, we "hired" Parker Thomas.

Parker was about seventy years old. He was a bachelor who

lived with an older sister. His needs for survival in life were modest. Given some new responsibilities, however, he rose to the challenge, and volunteered to work for us—doing anything he could do, for anything we could afford to pay. He was crippled by arthritis; still, there were lots of helpful things Parker could do.

"Crippled by arthritis" was no fib. This old man, after decades of heavy work dredging for oysters and handling fishnets, was bony, bent, and gnarled. The tasks of work on the water were no longer possible for Parker; yet he craved work, and all the sense of purpose that work lends to life.

And so we took him on—for the pittance we could afford. Practically speaking, Parker could still scull a skiff—could still take a small boat to the mail boat dock, and pick up the things we needed, and push them back over the waters to our own distant haven at Crab's Hole. He could help Henry to till the soil as he created a garden to feed his family. In due course, when the time came when we brought a pair of cows to our scene at Crab's Hole, our helpful Parker came to be known to his island friends as "The Janders' Cowboy." To us, however, he was always, simply, our Parker.

Parker was a character straight from the book of fantasy. He struck me as one of Snow White's dwarfs, initially the impression given by his bent arthritic shape. But then his cheeks were indeed round and rosy, and his head was quite bald. His ears drooped long. His eyes glinted, and hinted at his own private world.

His speech, too, was of another world, for he belonged to the rapidly diminishing number of older folk on the island who retain in their language the obsolete Elizabethan words that have been handed down to them through years of isolated living. The radio and the motorboat have brought the world to Tangier, and with it the speech of the outside world to the younger generation.

As each of us grew to love Parker, not only for his precious personality but for his qualities of honesty and utter dependability, for his moments of righteous indignation and in turn of naive enthusiasm, we were simultaneously entering into his affection as well. To the rest of the island folk we remained for many months outsiders.

Parker became our champion and it was due in no small part to his unswerving loyalty to us that we gradually became accepted as friends and fellow Tangiermen.

Parker loved coffee as much as I love tea. It became a ritual that some coffee was always on hand for him when he had finished the morning chores. Since he refused to be the slightest trouble to anyone I was compelled to assure him daily that the coffee was left over from breakfast and would be wasted if he didn't drink it. Thus reassured he would come in, take his customary place in the bay window by the table, drink his coffee with appreciative comments, reach to the window sill for the little ashtray I kept there for him, pull out a small bag of Duke's Mixture tobacco and roll a cigarette between his gnarled fingers. As for me, having finished the dishes, and in that first year of our residence on Tangier having scurried the children off to school and Henry to his building work, I poured out a fresh cup of tea for myself and sat down with Parker. The same procedure was repeated at three thirty in the afternoon, though then we were frequently joined by Henry. Then it was that we went traveling with Parker in his memory to the years of his youth. So vividly could he describe the events of his earlier days, and so precise were the similes which he employed, that I felt myself living in a different world during those precious tea-time hours. Many of his stories we heard again and again, but changed almost not at all. We followed him in his travels up and down the bay on fishing schooners, went with him by train with his fellow watermen to the west coast of Florida. Sometimes the children had milk and cookies with us, and they would spur Parker on to relate some favorite story.

"And now, Parker," one of the boys would coax, "tell us about the time you ate the devilled crabs down in Norfolk."

"I'll never forget that day if I live to be a hundred and twenty," Parker would commence. "Me and a couple of other fellows had tied up our boats and come ashore one night, and we were so thirsty we could have blotted up the biggest part of the bay. There was a place down there where they served ye these yere devilled crabs cheap."

"What are devilled crabs, Parker?" I would painstakingly remember to ask.

"Well, they take out the good part of the crab and mix it all up with a lot of fancy fixins and stuff it all back in. They're good, allright, and that night they tasted especially good. I got down three of four of them, and in between bites I was a-drinkin' beer. (In those days I used to take a drink now and then.) Well, before I realized it I'd drunk up a good lot of beer, and I began to fill up with gas. There just wasn't no end to the gas them crabs and beer give me. Why, when I'd belch, that gas would 'a kept an umberell afloat in the air without me having to touch its handle. Now that's gas, I'm tellin' ye. I never will forget that day."

"Tell us, Parker, about what Riz and Noah Crockett were famous for," Sylvia would beg next.

Beaming with delight, Parker would continue. "Now I remember well that Noah Crockett. He was the best hog butcher they ever had in these yere parts. He'd be a braggin' that he could take the innards outen a pig in one minute flat. The men would all come around when they knew that Noah was doing the killin', and they'd time him. As soon as they had that there hog strung up, they'd take out their time pieces and count; and, sure enough, old Noah would take just one good slit and have that pig cleaned out as pretty as you'd want to see. And he never did go over one minute, neither."

"And how about his father, Riz?" Henry would encourage Parker.

"I don't remember Riz so well myself, but they do say that he had the biggest callin' voice that ever was heard on this island. Why, the folks over in Canton said they had to quit work with their mules when Riz got his'n out in the field. Everytime he'd shout 'Haw!' to his mule the others over in Canton would stop dead in their tracks."

"I think we should call that big loud moaning sound that we hear whenever there is a northwester blowing, the ghost of old Riz Crockett," I said once after hearing the tale of the big voice of the old man who had lived at Crab's Hole many years ago. After this suggestion we never heard the strange sound without someone commenting, "There goes ol' Riz Crockett callin' to his mule!"

"Tell us again, Parker," Mark would ask, "about that ham sandwich you had on the train."

"I don't think you've got a knife here in this house that's sharp enough to cut a slice of ham as thin as that there ham was in that sandwich I bought oncet on a train goin' down the Eastern Shore," Parker would start obligingly. "When that man came along shoutin' 'Coffee and sandwiches!' I sez, 'See here, mister, give me one of them ham sandwiches': but before I paid him the twenty cents he wanted for it, I sez, 'You call this ham?' 'Sure, it's ham,' he sez, with an oath to it.

"What's the matter with it?' 'Well, I'd like to see the knife you cut this ham with, mister. Why this slice is so thin you could see Old Pint Comfort through it, in a fog'!"

This was the comment we were all waiting for, the comment that never varied—and never failed to bring us to gales of laughter. Parker knew that we were laughing with him, in appreciation of his gift for story-telling. He delighted in our laughter as much as we relished his tales.

Occasionally Parker would drift into reminiscences of boyhood days. Discipline, he said—"di-sci-pline" (with the accent on the second syllable)—was neglected in present days; yet, he felt, in his own childhood discipline was too much stressed. From this point on he would continue with tales of terrific switchings he had received from his teachers and from his father. These he suffered for numerous acts: from ignorance of his school lessons, or from stealing watermelons, or going swimming when told he shouldn't. This last offense brought many a beating from his strict father...until one night when Parker was out in the harbor in his father's boat, and fell overboard. Suddenly aware that his small son was missing, old Henry Thomas turned his boat about, and after what seemed to be a futile search, spied in the moonlight Parker's small straw hat, which had miraculously stuck to his head.

"When he pulled me out of that water, sob wet, wetter than a marsh hen in a high tide, I was cold as a month-old corpse. I had a swellin' on me forehead as big as a blown-up pig's bladder, where I'd hit the side of the boat when I fell over. My Daddy thought I was dead, as sure as anythin'; and after he got me home, and put me in bed, he went in his room and started prayin'. I laid there, a comin'-to, and I heard him prayin' out loud, 'Forgive me, Lord, for beatin' my boy for going swimmin'. If he hadn't a-known how to take keer of himself in the water, he'd a-drowned tonight. If you'll only let him live now, Lord, I promise, I'll never beat my son again.'"

"Some good came out of it for you, after all, Parker, if you didn't get any more beatings," I once said.

"Oh well, he never did beat me no more for swimmin', but there were plenty other things I did that he switched me for," chuckled Parker, rolling another cigarette, and laughing to himself. "We didn't any of us young'uns have it easy, back in them days. My sisters used to go out workin' for folks; and work they would, all week long, washin' and ironin', scrubbin' and cookin'. All they brought back with them on Saturday nights was fifty cents for their week's work. They didn't hardly get no two dollars to spend on foolishness on a Saturday night, the way youngsters do nowadays."

He would sit in thought for a time, sipping on his coffee. "We used to have a good time though, in spite of everything. On Wednesday and on Saturday nights we went courtin' in them days. Sometimes a whole crew of us would come together and have candy pulls in the homes of one of the girls. There warn't no parkin' on the marsh bridges then, neither," he assured me. "The girls had to be inside their gates at six o'clock; and if we didn't stand up well with their folks, we couldn't go courtin' them at all."

In spite of his regular attendance at candy pulls, Parker never did marry. With candor he explained to us that "the ones I could have got, I didn't want; and the ones I wanted, someone else got before me!"

As the months went along Parker became one of our family. We could have loved him no more had he been our "blood-kin," as they word it on Tangier. The children went away to school, since the curriculum in the school on the island was not geared for students aimed for college. When Sylvia and Owen and Mark wrote letters home, they addressed not just us parents, but Parker, too. When the children were expected home for vacations, it was Parker who met them at the dock with his skiff, to help with their bags. It was Parker's gleeful smile that said, "Welcome home!" Now that Parker is no longer with us, I myself can never approach the town wharf in the mail boat without seeing in memory his faithful presence, his bent figure leaning on the pole, waiting for our arrival.

Once Henry took Parker with him to New York on a sightseeing trip. Parker had been to the Big City before, on a couple of fishing expeditions, but had explored only a limited area near the docks. This time he visited Rockefeller Center and the Music Hall, he traveled on the subway and the old Third Avenue El, and he rode to the top of the Empire State Building—the highest place on earth where he'd ever been, he announced. This trip occurred on Navy Day weekend, so the city was particularly crowded. From the roof of the apartment house on Riverside Drive, where some dear friends of ours lived, Henry and Parker looked down upon the impressive river parade of America's Navy. For Parker, for whom boats and water were the basic things of everyday existence, this was one of the most thrilling days of his life.

Some months later Parker went with Henry to Washington, and thence down the Skyline Drive to Charlottesville, to the University of Virginia, where our eldest son, Kent, was then a student. Then back through Richmond and Williamsburg, to Norfolk, and home.

Henry took great joy in traveling with Parker. The old man savored every wonderful new sight, and was excited by history. Back home, on Tangier Island, Parker spent many an evening with his friends gathered in the store, recounting his adventures. No king ever reveled in his power any more than did Parker, as he held sway over his enthralled audience. For Parker the best of any experience was the joy of telling about it.

He had a quaint way of measuring the worth of a rare moment in terms of money. "To sit in that seat in that old Bruton Parish Church where Thomas Jefferson once sat was worth twenty dollars," he would say. "It was worth ten dollars to me just to watch people eating, way up there on the 86th floor of the Empire State Building. Imagine sitting way up there in the air, and just sipping on a Coca-Cola!"

Parker was not all sweetness; but his moments of indignation helped to make him the interesting character that he was. There had been children on the island who tormented him at times, as children have tormented their elders from the days of the Old Testament. Toward these youngsters he bore an abiding grudge; and when some of them tried to get his goat, Parker would grab for a switch and send them scampering in very real fear. For children who treated him kindly Parker's affection was boundless. When he visited New York he bought nothing for himself; instead, he came back laden with candy for Jerry and Freddie, Jackie and Jimmy, the children of his nieces.

Parker was especially proud of his collection of tools. On one occasion an elderly neighbor who had known him since his childhood dared to ask to borrow a favorite saw. "Now why can't she buy a saw of her own!" he grumbled to me. "I slaved hard to get the money together to buy that saw, and I've taken good care of it for years. I declare, I wouldn't lend it to my own grandmother." And he didn't lend it, either.

He was a creature of routine. As long as nothing happened to interfere with his regular attention to chores he worked with cheer but if a load of feed that we were expecting couldn't be picked up at the dock because of a low tide—and this delayed him in taking care of his other duties—he wore the dourest of frowns. At the same time, characteristically enough, he could not be prevailed upon to permit one of our boys to take over these tasks so that he could go home. "It's my job to feed the pigs, and I'll do it myself," he would announce glumly.

We learned soon enough, however, that if Parker was left alone in a "crisis" such as this, he would soon return to being his happy self.

The smallest things we did for him were tremendous acts of

kindness in his view. Since I frequently did my baking in the early afternoon I was often able to cut him a piece of warm pie, or a slice of cake, to go with his afternoon coffee. Later I would hear that he said to his cronies at the store, "Why, Mrs. Jander gives me the very first piece out of a fresh cake." Hearing such reports gave me chagrin that I didn't think of more things to do for him. So little meant so much to Parker. In return he couldn't do enough for us. If I chanced to be lying down for a catnap I sometimes heard him shooing away the neighbors' children as they paraded past our house on the way to the beach. When our children returned from school at Christmas time, he always managed to buy something special for them out of his meager savings—a big bunch of grapes, or a box of candy.

I never learned 'til after Parker's death that he had even overcome a strong dislike of cats, since in our home we always had at least a couple of cats.

So it was that Parker's coming to us was the most wonderful thing that could have happened to us in our new life on Tangier. He was our first intimate Tangier friend. Through him we learned the background of the people, from him we learned about their history. As he helped us to overcome the physical difficulties of life with its lack of conveniences, so he paved the way for us into the life of the island. For us there can never be another Parker.

BEFORE AND AFTER

THE HOUSE AT CRAB'S HOLE originally resembled nothing more than two big boxes attached to each other, the one slightly taller than the other. No shutters adorned the naked windows; there were no ells or porches to soften the severity of its high lines. It had been built by Severn Crockett, son of Noah and grandson of Risley, more than forty years previously, from materials salvaged from the ancient house of his grandfather, which had been located some hundred yards to the south. The beams and framework were very old, as were some of the floors. Henry, with his experienced eye, had said at once that the body of the house was sound and free from rot. By the time our family moved in, the lines of building had been changed significantly by the addition of baywindows on the south end of the living and dining rooms. These two baywindows were one long extension, and between them there was room for a tiny entrance hall and a small coat closet. The dining room-kitchen had been glorified by the addition of a built-in sink, counters, and cupboards along the entire northern wall, and the living room boasted a fireplace on the west—which was the only functioning fireplace on the island. (We have since learned that a number of the older houses of Tangier do indeed have very old fireplaces which have been plastered over as the more modern coal and oil-burning stoves came into popularity.)

The old floor in the living room we painted black; and, contrary to the advice of our neighbors, we didn't cover it with either a hardwood floor or the customary linoleum rug used on the island. As a result, we have suffered with cold feet in the wintertime; but we are able to point with pride in the summer to our original floorboards, and to delight in the beauty of their uneven surfaces, ridged from years of wear and sanding. Tangier houses cannot have cellars due to the costliness of making them waterproof, and so they are built on low piers of brick with an airspace left beneath to prevent rotting of the timbers. When a fierce nor'wester is blowing across the bay the wind sweeps through the cracks in the floor, lifting the small scatter rugs a full half inch above the old boards. By February of each winter we are almost persuaded that we should swallow our pride and succumb to the modernity of a hardwood floor. This past winter Henry came forth with a wonderful suggestion.

"Next summer when the boys are all home, Hon', we'll take care of this matter of the cold floors. I'll get some insulating material and they can wriggle under the house on their stomachs and line the floor from beneath."

"Do you think I should tell them of your idea in my weekly family letter?"

"Well," Henry answered speculatively, "perhaps it would be better to wait until they get here. Then, when they are eating your home-made bread and filling themselves with their beloved Italian spaghetti, I'll spring it on them."

Confidently Henry has bought the insulating material, beautifully thick, warm stuff; and knowing our boys and their love for Crab's Hole, we are trusting that they will acquiesce to this wonderful idea.

Only two people visited us the first summer we were at Crab's Hole. (This was another result of wartime gas rationing.) We weren't welcoming even the best of friends while we were in the throes of remodeling. Bob and Mary Lou, school chums of the children, did spend a week with us very soon after we arrived, however, and since they have visited us every summer since, have been able to pass judgment on each succeeding addition and improvement to the house. That first year we were completely paintless. The kitchen floor was without linoleum and showed evidence of having been painted in several different colors during its life's history. Every drop of water had to be carried from Miss Sadie's well because our cistern had been cleaned out upon our arrival, and it hadn't rained since. The gorgeous, green icebox had been acquired before Bob and Mary Lou arrived, but Bob was drafted to assist Owen in the hauling of ice, via wheelbarrow, over the mile-long trek from the dock, a procedure necessary at least three times a week. We had screens for the windows, but hadn't yet learned the art of keeping the house constantly sprayed, so that in a body we spent a full hour daily at the task of swatting flies. Our guests must have muddied their toes with Tangier clay, however, for they have returned each year, and their "ahs" and "ohs" of admiration at each new project accomplished between visits are a source of much satisfaction to the entire family.

Soon after moving in we built a two-story addition on the north of Crab's Hole, which gave us a large room upstairs. Ultimately, when Tangier gets its envisioned town water system, this will become a bathroom and storeroom; for the duration, however, it now houses a 900-gallon tank for the collection of rainwater from the gutters installed around the roof. The first floor of the addition is a summer kitchen, milk pantry, and general junk room. By gravity flow we are able to run water from the upstairs tank into the sink in our kitchen below, and into the little bathroom into which we converted the small closet under the stairs. In this tiny bathroom, along with a toilet and sink, we even have a shower, bought from "The Book" (as the islanders call the Sears Roebuck or Montgomery Ward mail-order catalogues). The toilet we use only rarely, since we discovered that it put too great a drain on our limited water supply.

We continue to take the journey to the little privy which stands in a lonely spot on the dike which encircles the Crab's Hole property. (This decision was made a rather general policy after one small visitor left the handle of the toilet ajar in the wee hours of the night, draining the storage tank almost to the bottom.)

Since the outdoor privy is inevitable we determined that ours at Crab's Hole should at least have individuality and a degree of respectability. Hence it was painted red with white trimmings to match the house, and within Henry built a neat little magazine rack to satisfy the peculiar habits of certain members of the family. On the south side is a big window offering an expansive view across the marsh to the distant shore of the Chesapeake Bay; and opposite that an equally large mirror. The little red outhouse we felt must have a name; and so we called it "Bermuda." ("I'm off to Bermuda!" is the family way of putting it.) Our privy is indeed an altogether private place; and since one of its finest views is toward the east—especially lovely in the early morning, at sunrise—we are all of us in the habit of enjoying our stays in Bermuda with the front door wide open.

On one occasion a mischievous guest stole up on Sylvia one summer morning and snapped a picture of her as she was off there in Bermuda. Roxy sent her snapshot to Sylvia along with a Christmas card; and Sylvia innocently opened the card in the presence of her latest boy-friend, who was spending his vacation at Crab's Hole. (We are now a bit more inclined to close that door behind us!)

While the painting of the interior of the house was left for later—and still isn't entirely done more than four years later—it was essential at the very outset that the exterior of the house be painted to prevent deterioration by the salt air and the hot summer sun. We chose red for its color, first because there were no other red houses on the island, and second, because red paint endures such climatic conditions better than other colors. The trim and the shutters we had added were painted white. The roof over the kitchen required new shingles and so we used white asbestos shingles to carry out the red-and-white scheme of the whole. The coffin-house, cowbarn, chickenhouse, and boathouse were painted to match.

"My gosh, from the Histing Bridge Crab's Hole looks just like one of those Currier and Ives prints," Kent remarked one day as he returned from a journey to the Main Ridge.

The first year's painting jobs were done principally by Henry and the boys, with Sylvia and me contributing dibs and dabs of labor. Preparation of meals for the hungry crowd, with every bit of food having to be carried from the Main Ridge, kept us females pretty busy, however. The outdoor work was producing appetites of amazing proportions.

To make the northern extension look right architecturally its roof was extended to include a small kitchen porch, but the construction of the brick floor for it was postponed. A year or two ago, all of the family being at home for six weeks or so, it was decided that the time had come not only to finish that brick floor but to build the long desired screened porch on the west end of the house, looking out toward the bay. The porch construction went along fairly rapidly, but the work on the floors of the two porches was a tedious task. First of all, the boys ferried sand in the skiff from the beach, making fully three dozen trips. While Owen and Mark took over the sand job, Kent did the excavating and the transferring of the topsoil gained thereby to the low areas of the lawn. Next he built a sustaining wall along the outer edge of the excavated area from concrete blocks surmounted by bricks. It seemed that the sand never would fill up the space, but at last it was time to lay the bricks. None of the boys had ever tackled such a job before, but under Henry's expert guidance they managed fairly well. Owen mixed the cement, stopping frequently to repair to the living room to listen to his beloved phonograph records, to Kent's utter disgust.

"Will you please make that brother of mine attend to business, Mother?" was a common request that summer.

Mark carried the bricks and Kent laid the floor according to a pattern worked out on paper. When the screened porch was finished its handsome brick floor had the proper slope toward the sides to carry away the rains that might beat in from the bay. The result was just beautiful! We could scarcely wait for the cement to dry between the bricks before moving in the porch chairs and the old homemade table and benches that had been patiently waiting in the coffin-house to be put back into use. A space was left in the floor of the west porch just directly in back of the living room fireplace for a grill, which was last summer's project, the most recent install-ment in the beautification of dear Crab's Hole. Now we are able to enjoy the hamburger roasts which had been prohibitive hitherto because of the uninvited guests, the mosquitoes. Incorporated into the grill are numerous stones that we picked up on our family camping trip of a year ago: a stone from the bottom of Salt Lake, one from the summit of Pike's Peak, another from the coast of Or-egon, and so forth. The focal point of the porch fireplace is a lovely tile on which is painted the only pleasant-faced crab we have ever seen (he actually smiles!). This jolly ceramic crab was the contribu-tion of our family dentist from New York, whom we have known for many years and, despite his profession, is among our closest friends. With Dr. Eolis as our guest we enjoyed the first frankfurters to be cooked on our new grill.

Over the baywindow in the kitchen there is a place that looked rather bare after we had completed the painting of the walls. It begged for something to perk it up, but pictures didn't seem quite right for the spot. "It needs a motto or a rhyme," we both agreed; but it was several days before we hit on anything to suit us. Finally I found a couplet by William Henry Davies; and Henry, with a narrow brush, lettered in blue the words which sum up appropriately our feelings as we sit together in the bay window lingering over our meals:

> "What is this life if, full of care,
> We have no time to sit and stare?"

Since painting episodes are being related, I must mention the blue morning glories, the dragon flies, and the hummingbirds which grace the walls of Sylvia's small bedroom. An artist friend of ours who was visiting Crab's Hole volunteered this contribution to the decoration of the house and spent a busy weekend with her brush. Having to leave on Monday, and being determined to finish her project before she left, she put on the final touches on Sunday afternoon. We had several callers that afternoon and had to resort to all sorts of deceit to conceal the fact that the Sabbath was thus being broken. We managed it, however, and Mrs. DuChene departed on the mailboat next day with an unblemished reputation. In spite of their Sunday application, the hummingbirds continue to sing, and the blossoms to brighten the walls of our daughter's room.

One of the reasons why it is fun to be poor is that one never can get all the work that an old house needs done at once. If it were possible to hire plenty of labor, and haul in materials without thought of cost, of course the rapidly attained results would be quite thrilling—but not nearly so much fun as when they are achieved in gradual steps. Each little closet that Henry builds for us, each coat of paint that goes on the walls, brings with it a special sense of achievement and joy. How much more pleasurable when things are not finished in one fell swoop—and there's always something new to look forward to. Already I am planning for an attic floor with a disappearing stairway, so that the parade of friends whom our children are always inviting can be more comfortably bedded down. I'd like a new fence for my rambling roses to grow upon, and a brick walk to the house with tulips bordering it.

The north field Henry wants planted entirely with fruit trees (it now has three pear trees, and some seedling pecans); and the south field he plans to have plowed completely to enlarge the garden, which is now rather small, since every bit of the soil must be turned over by hand. With the buying of a town tractor by the village council the chore of digging up the soil will be eliminated, and the big garden may become an actuality before long. We both wish to see the cowbarn—which no longer houses any cows—transformed into a small guesthouse. When these present dreams are accomplished, new dreams will doubtless take their place. By that time perhaps there will be grandchildren milling about the place, and already I can envision Grandpa building a playhouse for them under the fig trees.

THE COMING
OF THE COWS

P ARKER'S GNARLED FINGERS tapping on the window pane
brought me quickly from the kitchen.

"They're in sight, Mrs. Jander! If you'll come look you
can see them just alongside Watts Island." His face had its special
beam that appeared only on particularly happy occasions.

For an hour or more faithful old Parker had been patiently
watching, spyglass in hand, from the top of the lumber pile by the
boathouse, for signs of Willie Parks's boat. It would be easy to spot as
it made its way past Watts Island into the Tangier harbor, for behind
it would be the big scow that we borrowed from Cap'n Pete Williams
to bring over to Tangier the latest addition to our family, two big yellow cows. Yesterday Henry had gone over to Onancock, with our sons
Owen and Mark, to meet these new arrivals, promising to return next
day were the weather "pretty" (as we had now learned to say). Not a
whitecap had appeared all morning on either the harbor or the
bayside, so Parker was confident that early afternoon would see the
approach of Willie's boat. Now sure enough, his alert eye had spotted
the little white dot, followed by a larger one, on the horizon.

Slowly the dots increased in size as the boat made the turn from the harbor into the Big Gut; and we could plainly see the boys and Henry on board, and the shape of the two cows in their makeshift stall aboard the old scow.

"I do wish Sylvia would hurry home from the postoffice," I exclaimed to Parker, "so that she can be here to welcome the cows."

Scarcely had I spoken when over our bridge she ran, breathless with excitement. Following her were a dozen or more Tangier children. On the Main Ridge our daughter had been met everywhere with cries of, "The cows are coming, Sylvia! The scow's almost here!"

As we watched the boat drawing closer to the little canal that branched over toward Crab's Hole we could also see a long line of people making their way across the marsh road from the Main Ridge. The news of the coming of the cows, it seemed, had spread to every youngster on the island—most of whom had never seen a cow. For grown-ups as well this was an event, for there had not been a cow on Tangier Island for over twenty years. The path and the lawn were filled with excited and curious onlookers as the scow, now detached from the boat, was slowly poled by the boys up the canal toward the barn. Parker had been busily making ready, hauling planks to create a bridge so that the cows could get from the scow to the shore.

At last the scow was pushed to the very end of the canal, and the planks were laid down. Owen unleashed the larger cow, Beatrice, and led her to the improvised bridge; but when she glimpsed the water beneath the planks she balked—so abruptly that Owen and Parker alongside were nearly thrown overboard. A number of boys and men from the crowd on the bank (which was getting bigger by the minute), volunteered to push and pull; and this only increased Beatrice's fear, and her determination not to a set a single hoof on those planks. Henry quietly urged all the spectators to move off to a distance…and after a while Beatrice allowed herself to be coaxed over the bridge, where she was tied to a fencepost. From there she mooed loudly and nervously to her companion, Georgina, still on the scow.

Georgina was even more skittish and temperamental than

Beatrice. Sending the crowd back to an even greater distance was of no avail. Slaps on the rump did nothing to move her. A bucket full of corn was held where she could sniff it; but all she did was sniff it…and pull back in suspicion.

Then Owen took charge. On our small suburban farm in Connecticut we had had a couple of milkcows, so Owen had experience in these matters. Owen loved music, and always had music going in the background in the barn at milking time. Cows, he knew, have a special fondness for Mozart.

With one hand Owen gripped Georgina's halter; with the other he scratched between her horns; and into her ear he gently sang

Là ci darem la mano, / Là mi dirai di sì! / Vedi, non è lontano, / Partiam, ben mio, da qui. ("There we will join hands. There you will say yes to me. Look, it is not far away. My darling, let's go there.") —Don Giovanni's irresistible song of seduction.

Sure enough, Georgina moved cautiously across those planks and joined Beatrice on terra firma, whereupon the two of them were docilely led into the stalls of the barn, their new home at Crab's Hole.

From then on the affairs of the cows became part of daily conversation on the island, with Parker as the reporter of the news. Parker acquired his new nickname, "Janders' Cowboy." It was probably meant to tease; but this time he himself found it rather amusing and seemed not to mind at all.

The names "Beatrice" and "Georgina" were chosen as a distinct change from the typical bovine names that we had used for our cows in Connecticut: "Molly," "Buttercup," and "Daisy." "Beatrice" and "Georgina," I confess, were the names of a couple of my sorority sisters from my student days at N.Y.U. In a Christmas newsletter that I sent out that year I told the story of the Coming of the Cows on Tangier—and included the names of our new cows, and, of course, sent the letter to these two old friends. It would have been a faux pas save that both of these middle-age ladies were indeed very dear friends. They themselves had a farm in New York State, where they raised beefcows.

They wrote back reporting that they had just named their newest calves "Anne" and "Henry."

The regular scheduled hour for milking the cows soon became known to the children on the island; and when the cows had become thoroughly accustomed to their new environment, we permitted visitors to be on hand for this ritual. Mark, who formerly had attempted to get out of the milking chores, now sought the job. He sought it with such gusto, in fact, that I looked into the matter. I discovered that a considerable amount of cows' milk was getting squirted in the direction of visitors—occasionally into their open mouths.

We were besieged with questions. Till now we had been revealing our ignorance daily in our questions about the behavior of crabs and oysters. Now came our turn to be the providers of information.

"How often do you milk them?" "Why do you have to milk them every day at the same times; can't you just milk your cows whenever you need milk?"

Beatrice was "expecting"; and our neighbors were amused in some cases—horrified in others—when their children came home with new knowledge about this matter. Daily at school Mark was met with queries about Beatrice's condition.

"Mother says Beatrice looks as if the calf will come any day now," I was told that he reported. Finally the morning came when we found a sweet little bull calf snuggled up against Beatrice's great sides. Mark wolfed down his breakfast in record speed.

"Boy, will the kids be excited when I tell them the calf is here. I'll bet the teachers will have to close school!"

"All those children will frighten poor Beatrice and her calf to pieces if they descend on them today, Markie," I warned him. "You'd better tell them not to come down to Crab's Hole 'til Sunday. That'll give Beatrice time to calm down."

"Aw, heck," he protested, "they've been waiting so long to see a baby calf. Please let them come today."

Henry came to the rescue. "Sunday we'll have plenty of time

to take care of all the visitors, Mark. Two days won't make any difference in the size of the calf."

Begrudgingly Mark raced off to school with the news, and with the invitation for one and all to visit the new arrival on Sunday afternoon. That Sunday afternoon almost a hundred children came to view Beatrice's calf with awe and excitement. The calf was named Billy Carroll for one of the little boys up the lane who had shown unusual interest in the affair. This, we realized later, was not such a good idea, for when the day came that we had to butcher the calf, we not only ran into the problem of trying to sell veal in a community that ate beef and pork, chicken and seafood—but never lamb or veal—we also sensed that nobody wanted to eat "Billy Carroll." Our own family overcame its own sadness over the situation, and managed with little difficulty to enjoy an orgy of veal cutlets.

Since all six members of our family could milk, we found the chores connected with the care of the cows not too strenuous or confining for anyone. The whole adventure of having cows on the island turned out to be rather expensive, however, since Georgina and Beatrice had to be kept in the barn much of the time, for when they were left out in the pasture very long the flies nearly drove them wild. DDT hadn't yet become available; but with various sprays, and with tight screens on the windows, we were able to keep the barn free of flies. Another hindrance to putting the cows to pasture during the early months of spring was the presence of onion grass in the meadow. Unless the cows were brought in a good six hours before milking their milk tasted unpleasantly of garlic. To solve this problem we had to buy a regular supply of hay; and since no hay was available on the island, this all had to be brought over from the mainland on a boat. Hay, and grain, too—which ran up quite a bill. We were able to sell a number of quarts of milk each day to neighbors, who were happy to get really fresh milk. Only a small amount of milk was available in the Tangier stores because of the problem of inadequate refrigeration during the trip across the Bay, and the risk of the milk going sour. We could have sold huge quantities of milk. We gave priority to neighbors with children; but we always reserved eight quarts a day for our own family—not just for milk and cream, but for butter and cottage cheese, as well. (People on the island, accustomed mostly to canned milk, found it hard to imagine that a family of six could consume so much milk.)

Since electricity has come to Tangier, and really efficient refrigeration, the problem of the preservation of milk has been greatly eased; and so now fresh milk has become a much more common item in the diet of the islanders.

Another thing that made the cows so expensive was the business of breeding. It didn't pay us to keep a bull for just two cows; and our plan of making use of the method of artificial insemination proved impossible since we were not in an area where there was much dairy farming, nor were there veterinarians on the Eastern Shore who could assist us with this problem. Therefore, when it came time for Georgina—who had had a calf just a couple of months before being brought to the island—to be bred anew, there was no alternative but to carry her away on the same scow to a farm in Onancock, over on the mainland. When the proper day arrived for the voyage, again she balked at our efforts to get her onto that scow; and only when we decided to take Beatrice, too, would she go. Sylvia and Owen accompanied the scow and the cows, with instructions as to the location of the farm to which they would lead the animals upon arrival at the Onancock wharf.

"It's a good thing Owen was along. Mother," reported Sylvia when the two returned to the island. I never could have managed Georgina alone. She was so scared of the cars that were around the dock that she started to run away. Owen had Beatrice to look after, so I held as tight as I could to the rope."

"You should have seen how Sylvia held on, Mom," said Owen, very proud of his sister. "All the men around the dock said she was mighty strong. She fell down, but she still held on to the rope till I could get there to help her."

"Were you hurt, Sylvia?" I inquired with anxiety.

"Oh no, but pretty dusty. After I got brushed off we started down the road. They were quite well-behaved after that. When we reached the farm the folks there were surprised to see two cows instead of the one they were expecting. I explained about Georgina's being temperamental, and relying on the company of Beatrice. Those people knew all about cows, and understood. They even had a good laugh about the situation."

Since it was necessary to leave the cows for a couple of days, a second trip with the boat and scow was required. This time Sylvia and Owen reported that Georgina and Beatrice behaved most sedately on their walk from the farm back to the dock; and as time revealed, the journey to the mainland was a successful one. The following spring Georgina presented us with a daughter, whose cost, because of her mother's mainland visit, was considerably higher than the cost of calves in Connecticut, where we just walked the cows around the corner to the neighbor's farm—a total of $3, compared with the $45 bill in this case.

While the second calf was a bit of an old story to the children, still there was a tale in connection with its arrival which we have enjoyed. We had been awaiting its birth for several days. Parker said the cow just wouldn't have the calf unless we let her go out into the back brush to which she had escaped once already.

"That's where she wants to have that calf, and not in here," he affirmed. As days passed without any calf appearing it did look as if Parker were right. Finally we had some visitors from Connecticut, our former family doctor, his wife, and little girl. The doctor was to leave next morning to return to his patients, while the others were to stay with us for a couple of weeks. That evening little Toby joined Mark and the rest of us in making frequent trips to the barn to watch the progress of the birth of the calf, which had at last given evidence was about to happen. Dr. Ellrich himself—rather callously, his wife and I thought—urged us to let Nature take its course, which Nature did. Finally Georgina was happily licking a very nice little heifer. Next day Parker told around town that at Crab's Hole they do things right: they get a New York specialist down to look after their cows! The fact that Dr. Ellrich did leave the next day on the mailboat gave credence to the story, which was soon spread as gospel truth.

Beatrice grew too old for the trip across the Bay to the mainland, but without a new calf to encourage her milk supply she became a burden; and so she, too, had to be butchered. This time, however, meat rationing was in force, and we could have sold twenty Guernseys.

Carefully fed and tended by Parker, the cow's meat was remarkably tender, and many families who had watched her arrival on the island with interest now participated in her departure.

Then the Jander children, one by one, went away to school, leaving their father and mother with the confining task of milking Georgina twice a day without any hungry children to drink up the milk. Having found that even by selling the milk we could not keep a cow on the island profitably, and being unable to get anyone to tend to the milking when we occasionally went away on visits (the watermen's early departure to their crabpots didn't work in with milking hours), Henry and I decided that perhaps Georgina, too, had better not stay with us any longer. Georgina, however, had given twenty-five quarts of rich milk at the birth of her calf, and was still continuing to give nearly as much. It seemed a pity that her gifts shouldn't be appreciated, and so we managed to sell her and her now half-grown calf to a farmer who lived on the road to Salisbury, Maryland. Two years almost have passed since then, but we still stop by the fence of that farm whenever we drive along that road, to wave to Georgina as we see her grazing peacefully on the lovely green pasture there—where she is no longer tormented by flies. She doesn't recognize us, of course; still we are happy at the thought that other people are enjoying her good milk.

CHILDHOOD
ON THE ISLAND

H AD MY CHILDHOOD been spent on Tangier Island I should much have preferred to be a boy. The factors that make a small girl's life worthwhile and joyous are not a whit different here than on the mainland; there are plenty of old barns and outbuildings in which to play house, to be sure, and the narrow road is as satisfactory for playing hop-scotch as is any city street. But for the little boy the island is a true Paradise. Let me tell you about Jerry and his gang, whose days are typical of those of all lads on the island.

It has been fun to know Jerry—Jerry with his small round face decorated with large brown freckles, and with a vacant space in his rows of small teeth to prove his statement that he is "most six." Jerry comes regularly to Crab's Hole, rarely alone, but with his small gang which he rules through greatness of age—the others are only five or six—rather than through great daring. Jerry's courage, in fact, is really the spirit of adventure; it is not the stubborn fearlessness of small Jackie, next in size of the gang. Jackie is so shy that he has been heard to talk by few adults other than his mother; but under his mop of tight brown curls is a will that is daunted by nothing, not even by Cap'n Auss Daley of the *Josephine D.*, which plies its way regularly between Tangier and Washington's fish dock. Cap'n Auss wouldn't harm a hair of any child's head, as the older youngsters know; but he does enjoying chasing small boys. He met his match, however, in small Jackie who, when Jerry-the-Daring and all his other playmates ran screeching from Cap'n Auss, stood his ground fearlessly, to the huge delight of the Cap'n and the onlookers at the corner store.

Tagging along with Jerry and Jack comes Jimmy, the small brother of Jack, who can be told from him only by his lack of freckles. Bobby and Andrew, called "Andra" by the rest, live nearby and are important members of the gang. Where the others seem always to be either in the process of removing their shoes and stockings, or carrying them about in readiness for jumping into the canals, Bobby and Andra appear always as two small, smiling faces springing out of two pairs of huge rubber boots. Sometimes their group is increased by the presence of Billy Carroll, for whom our calf was named, and who plans (he tells me) to be a preacher someday.

Days are never dull for Jerry's gang. Early spring finds them searching the island's dikes and paths for the wild asparagus which grows in abundance on Tangier. Going "spar grassing," the boys call it. When each small boy has his hands full of the tender stalks, he ties a piece of marsh grass about his bunch, and together the little group starts out to sell its harvest. For just fifteen cents I can buy from them more than Henry and I can eat. The stalks are rather thinner and darker than the cultivated variety of asparagus to which we are accustomed in American stores; but the difference in flavor is similar to the difference between cultivated strawberries and those small tender wild strawberries which country folk pick for shortcakes and preserves. Wild asparagus is tender to the very base of its stalk, and needs only to be rinsed quickly and cooked the shortest possible time. It is a heavenly treat!

The pennies which Jerry used to make from selling his asparagus he was accustomed to deposit in his small bank, his mother told me. Too, whenever a neighbor sent him across the marsh to the Main Ridge to the store with his little cart, the pennies he earned he would carefully stick into his bank. But then came the temptations of the candy counter at the corner store...

This old store had formerly been run by Cap'n Willie Crockett, who in one period had been the mayor of Tangier. Cap'n Willie was one of the old-time citizens who will be remembered, as long as anyone who knew him still lives, for his firm stand on questions of right and wrong. Finally he was too feeble to continue running his store, and so it was closed.

But then it was bought by Jack and Jerry's parents, who restocked it with groceries. The re-opening of the corner store at the south end of the West Ridge was a great convenience for those in that part of the island, who no longer had to carry all of their groceries across the marsh from the Main Ridge. But alas for Jerry's little horde of pennies! At last report Jerry's bank has been getting lighter and lighter, his instinct for saving giving way to his love of lollypops and bubble gum.

When the asparagus season is over the boys take to the water. From the long natural canal—called the "Big Gut"—which cuts through the length of the marsh between the Main Ridge and the West Ridge, there are several smaller canals, called ditches by the Tangier folk, used by homeowners to facilitate the transportation of fuel and supplies from the main dock. These canals—which have been dug by the men on the island over the generations—even at full tide are not dangerously deep, and even at low tide usually have sufficient water to float a skiff or a rowboat. Almost any day when the weather is pleasant our small friends can be seen poling a little boat along one of the canals. Usually Jerry sits in the stern of the boat and sculls.

"Sculling" is a technique of propelling a boat using just one paddle and one hand. It looks simple enough; but it is an art which I defy any adult to imitate who was not brought up from childhood in a community of watermen.

From his vantage point in the stern of the boat Jerry issues orders to his crew. Little Jimmy and Andra, too small to be of much use, huddle in the bottom of the boat. When inadvertently they are stepped upon by Jack in his poling maneuvers one hears a loud "Git outa my wy!" followed by much screaming to which no attention is paid by the others, intent in their search for crabs. If Jack is poling, then it is Bob's and Billie Carroll's turn to catch the crabs in their nets. "Thar goes one!" shouts Jerry. Jackie tugs at his pole, and sometimes there is an excited shout as one of the small watermen pulls forth a wiggly mass of claws. Back into the water are hurled the Jimmy crabs and the peelers, which are useful only if taken to the crabhouses way out in the harbor, a journey which is taboo to Jerry's gang since it involves the crossing of deep water. The boys are out to catch the nice soft crabs which can be taken home immediately to be fried for supper. Sometimes Jerry decides the boat is too full, so little Jimmy and Andra must wade alongside. Their faces blissfully happy, and their little legs pushing bravely through the water, they spend long summer hours learning the business by which most of them will earn their livelihood in the years ahead. Young as they are, as they come home for their supper at the end of the afternoon, much disheveled, they often proudly carry with them a small catch of softies for the family frying pan.

All the island youngsters become expert swimmers. The West Ridge children hie to the Bayside when the sun becomes really hot, and without the formality of bathing suits they spend many happy hours in the water. Increasingly often they come for their daily swim in the deep swimming hole formed by the union of two canals near our cowbarn. There the water is deep enough at high tide for diving. Since no windows face the east on the first floor of Crab's Hole, the boys seem to feel sufficiently private, though they are but a hundred feet from the house. (Should one happen to be glancing out an upper window one can see their glistening little bodies in all their glory.) The fact that Henry and I permit them to swim in our swimming hole seems to have raised us considerably in the estimation of many of the youngsters.

"They don't keer whether we're naked or not," they assert with approval.

Main Ridge youngsters, unless moved to take the long walk to the bay, dive off the dock up at the harbor and swim among the various boats that are moored nearby. Apparently in days past it was only boys who learned to swim, judging from the scarcity of grown women on the island who have mastered the skill; but nowadays the barriers have been removed, and fully as many girls as boys can be seen on the boats that go over to the main beach north of the lighthouse, now cut off from the island by a channel, for a late afternoon swim. There, when the flies aren't too bad, they enjoy picnics and hotdog roasts in the custom of young people the country over.

When the winter is hard on the island—which is not very common—and when ice forms on the canals, Tangier becomes a second Holland with boys and girls skating on the canals and in the harbor. Most years it doesn't get sufficiently cold for this sport, but then the ditches still play a role in winter games. Then the boys take pleasure in jumping the canals. Many a day Mark has returned from school with muddy shoes and trousers soiled from misjudging the width of the canal he was jumping. This sport goes back to earliest days on the island, for they still tell about one Tangierman who could jump the Big Gut at one of its narrower spots. Never before or since, they say, has his feat been equalled.

Early Saturday afternoon sees a rapid disappearance of all children from the streets. It is time for the weekly bath. Around five or six o'clock they begin to emerge again, cleanly clad and with thoroughly scrubbed and highly polished faces. The younger children walk carefully along the roads, trying to remember their mothers' admonitions to keep clean, but often by eight o'clock, when all the sandwich and confectionery stores have done the usual Saturday night's thriving business, they return to their homes with signs of chocolate and icecream to mar their previously spotless appearance. The older youngsters have by then gravitated into groups of boys and girls, walking arm in arm up the street, singing joyfully and boisterously, some few couples standing affectionately close to each other against the picket fences. It is courting time on this little dot of an island in the Chesapeake Bay.

NEIGHBORS

N EIGHBORS, according to Webster, are those who live nearby. To write about our neighbors on Tangier would be, therefore, to write about everyone, for the most separated families are no more than a mile apart, and our lives are constantly touching those of the thousand or more other folk of the island. Still there are always some people whom we see oftener than others, either because of their very proximity or because of some spiritual kinship between us.

Almost every day I find it necessary to take the walk up West Ridge and over the marsh to the post office on the Main Ridge. In Tangier vernacular this is called "going over." Smiles of amusement used to appear on the faces of neighbors when we first came here and spoke of "going uptown;" but now, when we have errands to accomplish, we too "go over." If it is a pleasant day as I go I am sure to see a great many of the people who have taken their places in our hearts as neighbors and friends.

In the very first house beyond our Crab's Hole bridge live Willis and Stella May, with Miss Mandy, the mother of Willis. Stella May is noted as being one of the best housekeepers on Tangier, and when I first became acquainted with her it worried me no little bit when she came to visit me lest she see the multitudinous dirty places in my house. But as I came to know her better I realized that Stella May's concern was for her own house, not mine. As I pass by I watch her shaking out her dustmop or hanging snowy white clothes on her line, and I wish that I could be half the housekeeper she is. Her little daughter, Doris, who will be a second Stella May someday, and one of her small friends, come each Saturday morning to help me with household tasks since our children have left home for school. I am not sure whether it is fondness for me, or the small teaparty we have at twelve o'clock that makes these girls so faithful, but nine o'clock on Saturday finds both Doris and Evelyn standing at the back door, sleeves rolled up and ready for work.

Cap'n George Pruitt, who lives just a short distance up the lane, is quite old and rather deaf. He can no longer do the heavy work required of a waterman, but manages to eke out a small sum during the warm months by fishing a few crabpots, and during the winter months he stays close indoors by his fire while he skillfully fashions the wire pots for himself and for others who are too busy to make their own. On Cap'n George's face there isn't a single unpleasant wrinkle. Surely in his lifetime he must have had cross thoughts occasionally, but so infrequent and mild must they have been that they have left no trace behind to mar the pattern of the genial wrinkles on his countenance. Both Henry and I are very fond of Cap'n George, and when we catch up with him as we are walking along the path we slow our pace and raise our voices to accommodate the kindly old man. His wife, Miss Nora, is considerably younger than he, and is an authority on all the past happenings on the island.

"How're you feeling these days?" I inquire, if Nora is out in her yard.

"Not much, honey, not much," she is apt to rejoin. "My head kept me awake all last night. I'm going to try to go over this evening though; I need a few things at the store." Though a sufferer from numerous ailments Miss Nora braves the miseries of them all to attend church regularly and the meetings of her lodge.

Dear Miss Sadie lives just a little farther up the road. She is perhaps the oldest of our neighbors, and I like to drop in to see her when I can because she reminds me so much of my old Welsh grandmother whom I used too call Nain, the Welsh word for grandmother. There must certainly be some kinship between the Welsh and the Cornish who first settled this island, for there are so many people here who remind me constantly of the old Welsh settlers of Oneida County, in New York State, whence my parents came. Miss Sadie isn't very well and ventures forth from the house only when spring has definitely arrived; but she keeps a lively interest in everything about her house and, with the help of her small grandson, Ronnie, looks after a few chickens each year. She and I swap slips of plants, too, and when she comes down to have lunch with me, which has been only too seldom, I feel that I have been honored and blessed.

Cap'n Will Thomas is one of but two farmers on Tangier Island. For many years he has tilled several acres of land surrounding his house, which, with Crab's Hole and but one or two others are the only homes that can boast of any acreage other than marshland. From experience he knows what vegetables will grow on our soil, which is good but rather heavily salted at times. Our big boar consented to become the husband of Cap'n Will's sow last year, and this year there were a lot of little pigs up at Cap'n Will's place. Enclosed within a moveable fence which Cap'n Will changes to a new location every few days, these young hogs do a marvelous job of rooting up the wire-grass which is an abiding worry to gardeners in these parts, but which through Cap'n Will's ingenuity will this year be transformed into pork. Cap'n Will and I discuss the weather as I stop by his fence to watch him at his garden work.

"Unless that wind shifts around to the west'ard or the southwest, we won't get any pretty weather," he states pessimistically. "With that nor'west wind we can't get it warm. Bad for crabs, too," he adds with a shake of his head.

Over on the Main Ridge I rarely reach the post office without running into Cap'n Keaser, an Eastern Shoreman who married here many years ago and remained on the island. Cap'n Keaser is frank, and when he wants to know the answer to a question he just asks it—which is one of the reasons we like him so much, I guess.

"Just how old are you, Mrs. Jander?" was one of his first queries after I came here.

"Thirty-eight, Cap'n Keaser," I replied bravely and honestly, for such was my age at that time.

"You don't look it, ma'am, you don't look it. You sure are holding up well for your age." I am sure that I walked with a springier step as I left him.

"Say, is that old gentleman from the city who visited you last year comin' back again?" he asked me once. "He sure was a nice fellow. I liked him. What did you say his work was now?"

"He's a sculptor, Cap'n Keaser. He makes statues of people."

"Well, now, I never did know one of those before. Nice fellow, though!"

His cheery smile is never absent from his face, though he has been a great sufferer from diabetes and for a time was bedridden. Last winter he became converted, and each Sunday finds him hobbling with his cane to the church services. If I start forth from Crab's Hole with any worries tugging at me, and haven't met either Miss Nora or Miss Sadie to help me shake them off, Cap'n Keaser surely manages to take care of them once and for all.

There are many other Tangier folk whom I now feel are close friends, and some of them I meet on each trip I make. Often I come upon Lucy and Sarah, sisters who live just across the narrow little street from each other and who often are found chatting with each other across the fences. They always make me feel important for, as the Tangierman would say, they "brag on me"—which really means that they give me compliments. Sometimes there is time for me to take the little sidetrip over to the section of Tangier called Canton, a little hamlet to the east of the Main Ridge and separated by its own stretch of marshland. I can never hope to get back to Crab's Hole from Canton in less than several hours. Though separated from me by a mile or more, there are folk over there who are as close to me as my neighbors down near Crab's Hole. Miss Emmy I usually call on first. Her son was an officer in the Marines in the First World War, and on her mantel rests proudly a delightful little group of Dutch dolls in Delft-ware, brought to her by him from Holland. Miss Emmy must have been beautiful when she was young; she still has curly hair and eyes that look out from a soul that is alive to the fun of the world. She always tells me funny stories about her childhood over which I giggle to myself all the way home across the marsh. Her sister lives near her and is a chronic invalid, having been shut in about fifteen or more years. Married a second time to a man fortunately younger than she, she is blessed in having his faithful and gentle care; and she pays for his care, without realizing it, by the very vitality of her strong personality. Last summer one of her four splendid sons, all married and owners of good boats by which they earned a good living, died very suddenly. Charlie's death was as much a loss to the whole island as it was to his elderly mother, for his was an ever developing mind. The progress of Tangier was of great importance to him. Sometimes when we were overcome with pessimism at the seeming hopelessness of getting the towns-folk—who are individualists to the very bone—to work together in a spirit of cooperation, it was Charlie whose optimism spurred us on. And so, when dear Miss Julie, with great sobs, confided to me her fear that Charlie might not be among the "saved," since he had not formally declared his allegiance to the Methodist Church, I trust that the fervor of my assurance that a loving God must surely have welcomed home the big-hearted Charlie may have helped to soften the edge of her sorrow.

At Estelle Crockett's, still over in Canton, I try to end my visit to that part of Tangier. If I begin my visit there I never get farther than her door. She is a born hostess, quickly setting at ease all who cross her doorstep; and I sit there and eat of her good clam chowder or other good dishes until my conscience troubles me and I hurry home, always, however, carrying with me some choice morsel of

Estelle's cooking for Henry's supper. Estelle was one of the mothers who lost her firstborn son on the battlefields in Italy. The strength of her faith in the hereafter and her tremendous sense of duty to her husband and her remaining children has made her, as a result of her grief, a stronger figure than ever in her small community of neighbors who look to her for advice and strength in their own lesser problems.

If I haven't tarried too long in Canton there may be time just to say "Hello" to Esther Wheatley. Everyone on the island likes Esther. It isn't because she flatters folk, for she is inherently honest and speaks her mind, often plainly. She isn't very strong and she has a great deal of work to do in her home. Added to her regular duties she has the task of being the island's Larkin agent, a wearing job with its weekly collections of small amounts of money. Sometimes her kitchen is not entirely tidy, with the innumerable chores that Esther faces each day, but nobody—not even the most immaculate Tangier housewife—cares about that. We all go to see Esther. Esther and her husband went with us on a camping trip to Florida last winter, and in our close life together for two or three weeks I tried to analyze what it was that draws folk to her. Henry and I both agreed that it probably had to do with her very truthfulness and honesty. In a village where by its very isolation and its closely knit social life, gossip and sometimes deceitfulness have ripe soil in which to thrive, it is heartwarming to find the Esther Wheatleys, whose word is as dependable and as fearless as the prophets of old.

Down on our point of land we have other neighbors we have learned to know as the months pass by all too rapidly. South of the Canton hamlet and separated from it—as is Crab's Hole separated from the rest of the West Ridge—is a little house in which until a few weeks ago resided the oldest man on Tangier, and his wife. I met his wife once when I ventured to walk down that far, and she told me that from her window she could tell when I was hanging out my clothes on the line. Thereafter, whenever I was engaged in that most tiresome task, I found it fun to pick out the brightest colored clothes to hang on the line that could be seen by old Mrs. Dize. I felt that I was thereby saying, "Good-morning, neighbor!" Both she and her husband have passed away recently, but I never fail to think of her whenever I am pinning my clean clothes on the line.

Once when we were lucky enough to be taken by boat out to the lighthouse which is at the very tipmost southern point of the island, perhaps two miles from us over marsh, sand, and shallow water, the keepers there told us that they watch our light each night. It is distinguishable from the other lights of Tangier because of being somewhat separated; and since our house faces the south there is almost always a light in one or another of our windows that is visible to them. Now when Henry or I put out the lights as we get ready for sleep we feel that we are saying good-night to another neighbor, the keeper of the Tangier lighthouse.

GUESTS

C RAB'S HOLE—paintless, screenless, waterless, and ice
less—was scarcely a place to which to invite guests.
The first summer of our life on the island, therefore, was
also guestless, except for the visit of Mary Lou and Bob, teenage
friends of our children who could be counted on to enjoy ten days
of roughing it. Gas rationing helped to accomplish this guestless
condition. These last three years, however, have more than made up
for our isolation during that first summer. While many of our Connecticut and New York friends found it a great effort to manage
their first visit to our island, the majority of them who found their
way to Tangier have returned. Our Crab's Hole guestbook now has
the names of almost a hundred friends in it, and many of the names
found there are found again a second, third, or even a fourth time.

There are some friends from earlier years—very dear friends
—whom we thought it wisest not to invite to our home on Tangier.
These are people who would not appreciate having to walk a full
mile to get from the dock to our home at the far end of the island.
People who would not realize how essential it is to use water
sparingly—very sparingly. People who could find no charm being

in a house without electricity. People—above all—who would be uncomfortable "making a trip to Bermuda."

"Bermuda," as I have explained, was our name for Crab's Hole's outhouse toilet; and "Bermuda" was really quite jolly—as even some of our "civilized" guests had to admit—what with its brick-red exterior with the white trim, and its cheerful whitewashed interior. Not only did "Bermuda's" huge glass window afford a wonderful, and yet very private view across the marshes to the Chesapeake Bay beyond, in dizzy contrast, its other walls were decorated with color photos of the Rocky Mountains. And then, there was that magazine rack. When guests at Crab's Hole took "a trip to Bermuda," they often were gone for the longest time!

Another fact of life on Tangier Island that gave us pause whenever we thought of friends whom we wanted to come visit, was the presence of mosquitoes. When the weather was dry, and the winds were brisk, mosquitoes were no problem. But Crab's Hole was surrounded by marshes; and when we had rain, and the air was calm, the mosquitoes rose in clouds. The approach to our house at the far end of the island led one through a screen of high marsh bushes. We learned to love this passage, for as one emerged from the thick growth, there, ahead, was Crab's Hole!

We also learned, however, that if the moment was right for one of those clouds of mosquitoes, here was a stretch for running. The attack was well nigh terrifying! Friends from Manhattan? Well, in the summer months, one invited only those friends with a predictably high tolerance for adventure.

Just getting from New York City to Tangier is an adventure in itself. We have set up a regular ritual for the arrival of guests. The mail boat for Tangier leaves Crisfield at noon. The one daily "express" train from New York which leads down into the Delmarva Peninsula links (at Princess Anne, Maryland) to a very "non-express" train from Princess Anne to Crisfield. This very local choo-choo, however, arrives at the Crisfield dock at two o'clock in the afternoon. That can well mean spending the night in Crisfield—which can be a quite charming experience unto itself. Crisfield, after all, is the "seafood capital of the Chesapeake Bay!" With a bit of luck, however, an imaginative traveler can usually pick up a late-afternoon ride over to Tangier with one of the island's accommodating watermen. With most of our guests from up north, on the other hand, we ourselves simply take the mail boat over to Crisfield, drive up to Princess Anne to meet them at the train there, and bring them home to Tangier without all that unaccustomed worry. Indeed, we have never failed to find a Tangier friend at the dock—always delighted to give us and our guests a ride out to the island.

Usually one or more Tangiermen could be found drinking coffee in one of the several eating spots around the dock. We always tried to find the friend who would be leaving first (or who had the fastest engine). Norris Angle's boat is a favorite with late-afternoon travelers to the island, for his engine is powerful, and he loves to push his boat along. By late afternoon we are always glad to be able to make the crossing of the Tangier Sound in as short a time as possible.

Some of our visiting friends come from New York by automobile. To reach Crisfield by noon means leaving the city around four a.m.! Rather than that, we advise people to start the trip from New York in the afternoon, stop off in Dover, Delaware (and enjoy the charming historical area of that old town), and then make a leisurely drive to Crisfield, in time for the Tangier mail boat. Even then, we like to go over to Crisfield to meet them, to help them find a place to park their car, and to give them a quick tour of the dock area there, as a prelude to Tangier.

Since the long walk from the Tangier dock down to Crab's Hole is indeed an impossibility for some of our older guests, we were accustomed, during Parker's years with us, to have him meet us at the wharf with his little skiff. Filled with satisfaction that he could be thus helpful, Parker would pole our friends, and their suitcases, along his own familiar route—through Rubens' River, and the Big Gut, and into the ever smaller canals to our home—talking with them, to be sure, the entire trip. (Now there's the way to be introduced to Tangier Island!)

Nowadays, bringing guests from the wharf down to Crab's Hole falls to the lot of one of our boys if it is their vacation time (Henry is not too adept at poling a boat) or to one of the Tangier youths who may be looking for a chance to pick up some change. Should our visitors wish to walk to Crab's Hole, Parker assumed the responsibility for their bags, and by the devious water route usually managed to reach our barn by the time we had completed a slow, meandering walk through the village.

It is always fun for us to watch the reaction of people on their first visit to the island. Although our young nephew, Yorke, had probably been told that Tangier lacked modern conveniences, it had apparently made no impression on him until he walked down the Main Ridge for the first time.

"What, no electric lights? Why, how do you cook?" he exclaimed. Then, as an afterthought, he added, "Oh, by gas, of course!"

Usually, however, folk from the mainland are so enchanted by our narrow streets, the picket fences marking the small lawns, the sunbonnets framing the faces of our women, and above all the lack of automobiles, that they forget for the moment the inconveniences of our life.

Arrival at Crab's Hole always means a cup of tea or coffee to rest from our walk—and that used to mean coffee with Parker. Those of our guests who knew Parker, and who shared in his genuine hospitality and eagerness to make new friends and to learn more of the outside world, agree with us that theirs was a rare privilege. Henry and I were once amused to have Parker say to us when we were expecting a new group of friends, "Do these people talk English?" Checking back we suddenly realized that we indeed had had a number of guests whose speech might seem foreign to Parker: Henry's mother with her strong German accent, two friends of English origin whose Oxford pronunciation had intrigued Parker, John Osimanti whose Italian turn to the English language was quite unintelligible to the uninitiated, a Bostonian, and several New Yorkers. So while our friends were in their turn enjoying the richness of Parker's vocabulary, we chuckled to think how their own speech mannerisms were tickling his own fancy.

One of the dearest of our old friends, Roxy, managed to get her toes so well covered with mud on her first visit that she has returned on several occasions. Roxy is the perfect guest—the one who enjoys herself under all circumstances, and for whom I never bother to tidy up the house. Not only do we enjoy her sunny ways, but somehow she manages to let us feel that we are giving her the time of her life. Perhaps it is coincidental that something unusual always seems to be connected with her visits to us. The first year that she came Roxie was on hand for the birth of the calf—the one that attracted eighty-six visitors on its first Sunday in this world. The next year she witnessed our first very high tide, when we were afraid that she wouldn't be able to return to her job in Connecticut. Another time we just happened to be going to Williamsburg when it was time for her visit; so we shortened her stay at Crab's Hole so that she might join the multitude of people who have admired the old Virginia capital in its restoration. Last year it was on Roxy's journey to Tangier that fate fell. We were driving her down with us from New York when the Buick, which at present writing has traveled well over 200,000 miles (climbing Pike's Peak at 180,000) had one of its now frequent spells of weakness and broke an axle somewhere in Jersey.

Not only do we ourselves enjoy Roxy's visits to Tangier, we have learned that many people on the island have come to look forward to her visits here. This fall, in fact, when Roxy was unable to come to the island because of the ill-health of her mother, there was actually a gloom on the faces of all to whom I told this sorry news.

Among those who felt that our move to Tangier might prove to be a mistake were Jean and Max. Jean is an authority on parent education and when, after three years, she and her equally busy husband were at last able to spare some time for us and Crab's Hole, she agreed to talk to our small and struggling Parent's Group. The contagious spirit of Tangier caught her, too, as the women who heard her speak flocked about her for advice on their problems. We now believe that she and Max may come again to visit us.

One difficulty about having company on Tangier, of course, is that visits are of somewhat longer duration than the customary short weekend stay of friends in the metropolitan area. In Connecticut I was able to put my best foot forward, to have my house neat on the surface, and to have meals planned ahead so that all ran smoothly. When guests are around the house longer than a weekend they usually ask to help with the housework, and so the weaknesses of my housekeeping crop out. Unpolished pans tucked away out of sight are always found by someone who is helping with the dishes; the broom that has needed replacing for months is inevitably pulled out of the closet; while somebody always wants to mend a tear, and my sewing basket in its ghastly tangle of threads has to be brought out into the open. No matter how hard I try to take care of such weak links in my efficiency before the arrival of guests I am never able to find them all, and the one weak spot I have missed is invariably the one which is discovered.

On the other hand the only methods of entertaining guests at Crab's Hole are those which involve real companionship. Walks on the island, a trip to the beach, perhaps a boat ride, sitting by the fireplace in the evening...these simple activities afford much opportunity for the interchange of ideas and opinions. When our guests have departed on the early morning boat for Crisfield (we let them trust to their own resources to get away from Tangier) and when Henry and I are alone again and are chatting over the visit just past, we frequently remark that we have learned more about So-And-So than we had ever known before, and that our friendship with him has grown in the few days he has been here. Just as down here we are much more aware of each tiny cloud that appears in the great expanse of sky above because there is nothing to hide the sky from us, so here in the quiet of Crab's Hole we are able to attain a spiritual closeness with our friends and to learn more of their inner selves when our communion with them is undisturbed by the excitement of the world we knew of yore.

Sometimes guests, observing the needs of the island and of the Jander family, have sent most welcome packages to the island on their return home. Some of the packages have contained books for our new town library. Often good old chewy pumpernickel bread, something unheard of on the island or on the Eastern Shore, but relished by the Janders, is sent us by our city friends. One guest, Stewart Heilman, wittily expressed his gratitude for his visit to Tangier by sending us our first can of that miraculous stuff, DDT!

THE WIND'S THE WEATHER

T HE WIND'S the weather," they say on Tangier. In Connecticut we lived totally unaware of the wind unless a hurricane were waging, and then I wouldn't have known whether it was a nor'easter or a nor'wester. Here the barometer is more important than a fever thermometer, and the slightest shift in the direction of the wind currents is sufficient to cause prolonged discussion among the men in the stores in the evening.

Seldom does Tangier's temperature rise to the extreme in summer that Baltimore, a hundred miles to the north, attains. Tempered by the surrounding salt water and fanned almost constantly by breezes, the island boasts of a climate that, while humid, is usually delightful and always endurable. Occasionally a day appears when our best and most faithful ally, the Southwest Wind, forgets us for the greater part of the daylight hours. Without fail, however, he appears again as the sun is fading on the horizon and stays to flutter the sheets if we sleep near an open window at night.

Tangier's marshland has its persistent occupant, the mosquito. The wetter the summer, of course, the more Tangier folk are pestered by them and by their meaner kin, the tiny gnat. Sometimes when it seems like too great a feat of endurance to fight the insects, and we are tempted to stay home from church on a Sunday evening, the breezes put forth more vigor and would seem to be assisting the Lord in their attempts to blow away the buzzing enemy. Since the southwest winds are prevalent in summer this works to our advantage, and while the trip up to the village must be made with a slap to each step, the return is made against the wind and scarcely a bite does one feel.

Though in summer the wind becomes our benefactor, in winter it is our foe. True enough, the thermometer here rarely drops below twenty degrees above zero, which to hardened Connecticut Yankees is as nothing; but when even that mild temperature is accompanied by considerable dampness and by a forceful nor'wester or nor'-easter, one's bones turn to icicles and one's blood to icewater after the mile-long trek across the marsh. Houses on Tangier, in generations past, have been built for the ten mild-weathered months of the year. They are single walled, with no sheathing—and our house is no exception. Hence, when it is a nor'easter that is chilling us, we hurry through breakfast in our easterly kitchen, and for the rest of the day stick close to the living room fire. When a day or two later the northwest wind sends out its icy blast we shun the living room with its single floor and abide in the kitchen.

Although this wintry wind is disastrous to our comfort, from another angle it is our friend, particularly when the thermometer hovers about freezing for a considerable time. Then it helps to prevent the ice from forming on the shallow waters that surround the island. Let the wind go down at such a time, and we wake in the morning to find Tangier Island cut off from the outside world. In the winters of 1917 and 1935 there were weeks that passed before boats were able to cut through the ice of the sound channel. In 1917 the ice covered the entire Tangier Sound and people were able to walk upon it from Crisfield to the island. Food supplies became low; and had a serious illness developed at that time it would have been a disaster. In 1935 the island's plight was known to the mainland as a result of airplane flights, and food was landed to tide over the emergency. Too, during that freeze an appendicitis patient was flown to a Washington hospital barely in time to save the boy's life. Nowadays, with the advent of radio telephone we are able to make contact with the Coast Guard at Norfolk, and an ice cutter is sent to break a welcome path through the impacted ice.

Last winter the wind played a strange trick on the island. There had been a freeze of short duration, but a thaw came soon after the cutter had appeared to relieve the situation, and it seemed that the freeze was over. Therefore, another Tangier housewife and I went to Crisfield and thence to Salisbury to shop. We arrived in Crisfield too late for the last Tangier boat and spent the night in the new home of a former Tangier resident. Next morning we shopped a bit more and reached the dock just before mail boat time. To our amazement there was no Tangier boat. Our watches said that we were ahead of time, so surely the Cap'n couldn't have left us behind. The harbor before our eyes was entirely free of ice and we were definitely incredulous when a man on the wharf informed us that Tangier was frozen in and no boats had come over. Telephoning to Homer Williams's store on Tangier I learned the details. The ice had broken loose from the upper bay, and on its trip southward through Tangier Sound had suddenly shifted into Tangier harbor, driven by an unpredictable change of wind. There the ice had piled up and formed a complete barrier. We stayed not only one more night, but several, before the cutter came once again in response to the petitions of the mayor of the island to break again the obstructing ice mass.

In the fall of the year with the equinoctial storms and extremely high tides, life on the island is again uncertain. Hurricanes meandering crazily up the coast from the West Indies and Florida usually spend themselves by the time they are as far north as Chesapeake Bay; or else they have veered out to sea. The islands of the Chesapeake Bay seem protected from the greatest violence of such tropical storms, even if they do retain a measure of destructive capacity in their northward route. Only once in the memory of the oldest folk on Tangier has the island felt the impact of a truly severe storm. That particular one is referred to as the August Storm. It came in 1935. A period of heavy, drenching rain preceded this infamous storm. In the powerful gale that followed, a sudden change of wind from the southeast to the northwest—bringing with it an extremely high tide—forced the water of the Bay itself over the island, and created havoc. One solitary spot on Tangier, in the section called Canton, was the only place not covered by the tide. Scarcely a house escaped water covering the first floor. Chickens were drowned, gardens ruined, and saddest of all, the trees that had lined the narrow streets were practically all torn up by the roots. Today Tangier boasts only a few tall trees, and it will be years before its streets are again blessed with shade.

Islands, especially flat ones like Tangier, fare better in high water than the mainland, however. There is no high land against which the water can back up. The tide simply passes over the island. Not even in the August Storm was the water sufficiently deep to wash away any homes. Boats, however, were torn from their moorings and cast up on the shore, many of them damaged and all involving much expense and hard work before they could be returned to water.

The tide came into Crab's Hole house at that time to the depth of fifteen inches, we were told by the former owner. So it came about that in 1945, when we experienced our first really high tide and the water crept closer and closer to the house—reaching the first step, and then the second—we became panicky. Fortunately the weather was warm. Roxy was visiting us at the time, and she joined us as we waded barefooted, the water above our knees, to the boathouse where the feed for the cows, pigs, and chickens was stored. Hastily we raised the bags onto quickly improvised racks high enough, we prayed, to escape the water. Next we turned our attention to the house. Rugs were taken up, books on low shelves were piled onto tables, and everything found in low cupboards that might be damaged by the flood was lifted up onto counters...and when the last article was out of danger, we looked out of the window and beheld, almost to our disappointment, that the water was slowly receding.

It has happened on occasion that we have been caught, either at church or on a visit to the home of a Main Ridge friend, by suddenly rising tides. Luckily it has never yet been very cold when this has happened and so, removing our shoes, Henry and I have waded across the marsh road, feeling quite pioneerish and very, very brave, back to the rescue of the livestock at Crab's Hole. Once we got home just in time to rescue two of Cleo's small kittens who were taking refuge on the sills under the house. Their little tummies and toes were wet, but otherwise they were unharmed. Except that we have lost two or three hens to the floods at various times, we have escaped unscathed. Now we both have boots that are hauled out in September. At first Henry alone had them, but after he had carried me through the high water on his shoulders a few times he discovered handily that Mark's boots were the right size for me. Mark was away at school and didn't need them, Henry rationalized; and so the boots should be mine. Since they weigh so much that I am exhausted after a short distance I resort to them only when strictly necessary—which is when Henry refuses to carry me on his shoulders.

Because of the annual dip in salt water that a large part of our land receives there are a great many flowers that I simply cannot grow, not being blessed with a green thumb. One spot in particular, just below the bay window of our kitchen, seems to be particularly cursed. I have discovered, however, that roses don't seem to be too much disturbed by an annual dosage of salt, and this year I am attempting to grow some floribundas in the fatal spot. It is too early yet to prophesy their fate, but I have my fingers crossed.

In the autumn of 1944 we received the tail end of the Florida hurricane that damaged the Atlantic City boardwalk and caused some destruction even in New York and Connecticut. Visiting us were a sculptor and his wife from New York, who had spent their honeymoon year on a small island in the Bahamas. Loving the sea and its whims they were as excited as we to behold the fury of the wind. The old twisted cedar tree in our yard leaned so far in the wind that we feared that at each new gust its trunk might snap.

Surrounding the yard were several fig bushes, and these, with their rubbery stalks, were bent right to the ground.

And then we experienced one of Nature's most amazing phenomena: the "eye" of the storm! Suddenly the wind stopped. Above us opened the blue sky. The calm that set in for about twenty minutes was a moment of eeriness such as none of us had ever experienced before.

But then, just as suddenly, the blast resumed! The cedar tree again began to lean, and the fig bushes again were driven to the ground—but now in the opposite direction.

We couldn't waste much time exclaiming over the storm's beauty, for this time the wind was accompanied by furious sheets of rain. Every old blanket and towel in the house was pulled forth to sop up the floods that were coming into the place. At each northwest window, upstairs and down, one of us was stationed with a pail and a blanket to soak up the rain as it literally poured through the cracks. The walls themselves were drenched—how we wished right then for a sheathed house!—and when the storm had spent itself, our strength, too, was gone. Mrs. DuChene took to bed to rest after heroically doing her share. Her husband, followed by Mark and Owen, decided to walk to the beach to inspect the waves that were still pounding on the shore. Where we now have a sturdy little arched bridge over the canal there was still at that time only a plank. Our guest, misjudging the power of the wind, unwisely looked back for a moment as he crossed gingerly on the precarious bridge. The wind caught him off balance and neatly blew him into the waist-deep water. Owen rushed to Mr. DuChene's assistance; but Mark, after one glance to ascertain that he was not drowned, turned on his heel, ran back to Crab's Hole, took the stairs in a couple of leaps and burst into Mrs. DuChene's room.

"Your husband just fell overboard," he announced triumphantly. Thus it was that the rest of us greeted the dripping sculptor at the door with horror mingled with chuckles. It was one storm whose power he had definitely measured.

THE DEATH OF PARKER

FOR THE FIRST TIME in our married life Henry and I found ourselves alone a couple of years ago. Mark, our youngest, had left the roost to follow his older brother and sister to school in Massachusetts. Until Christmas time we managed to keep busy enough, and that holiday season was as joyful a one as we had ever celebrated, with all of our youngsters home once more at Crab's Hole. For over two weeks the old house shook its sides in accompaniment to the laughter and merrymaking within. Then the children were gone again, and ahead of us loomed the long and lonely months of winter. Building comes to a standstill on the island in the cold weather. It was the year when we were waiting for the transformers for the new electric plant, and it seemed useless and unnecessary for us to remain in Crab's Hole when the roaming-sickness was troubling the two of us.

We had once promised an acquaintance of ours who owned a gift shop and overnight guest house in Williamsburg that we would help her out some winter while she went to Florida. Her beautiful old home, one of the oldest in the town, was in need of interior painting, and part of our arrangement with our friend was that

Henry should redecorate some of the enormous rooms during our stay in her historical house. This seemed to be the logical winter for us to leave, and since the desire to savor the restoration of the old capital city without the haste of our earlier visits was strong in both of us, arrangements were soon completed. Parker agreed to stay at Crab's Hole to keep the pipes from freezing, and to look after the chickens, Cleo and Maedchen, and the one pig that was to go un-slaughtered till spring.

We felt that Parker welcomed our jaunts to the outside. He was a bachelor who had always made his home with relatives, who were always kind to him and welcomed him in their midst; still he enjoyed the pleasure of having a "home" of his own. Crab's Hole became Parker's castle, to exaggerate considerably, when we were gone. At his request the upstairs bedrooms were closed off, as well as the living room, and the kitchen-dining room was the only room that he inhabited. The old couch therein served as his bed, and in that one room he slept, cooked, ate, and read at the table in the bay window during the long winter evenings. With the cupboards well stocked, Parker could get his own breakfast and evening suppers, while for his mid-day dinner he went to his sister's home, a quarter of a mile up the West Ridge. This time we left behind for him to enjoy one of the smoked shoulders of the pig we had killed in the late fall. On Saturday afternoon when Parker left for home I assured him that all was in readiness for our Monday morning start; and, promising to be on hand early Monday to pole our bags to the dock, Parker bade us what turned out to be his last farewell.

Monday morning, for the first time in our friendship with him, Parker failed to appear. As time for the mail boat to leave neared, we piled the bags into the old cart and pushed them ourselves up the Ridge, stopping at Parker's home to inquire what had happened. Miss Adney, his sister, said that Parker was still in bed. He had suffered an attack of indigestion on Saturday night, she explained, and wasn't feeling well. But he was better, and would be able to go down to Crab's Hole later in the day. We promised to send a boy down to help Parker for a day or two, and arranged to telephone a day or two later to find out how everything was. This we did, after we were well settled in our new stopping place at Williamsburg. Miss Amanda, to whom we talked, relayed to us Parker's message that he was now much better, that everything at Crab's Hole was well, and that we should not worry. And so, with utter confidence in Parker who had never failed us, we didn't. Friday morning Miss Amanda called us again, this time to tell us that Parker had died.

Fortunately our friend in Williamsburg had not yet left for Florida, and we were able to return to Tangier immediately. On the boat next day we heard the details, Every Friday morning Parker had been wont to visit the little town barber shop. Unable to shave himself because of his crippled hands he went unshaven through the week and on Friday without fail appeared early at the shop. This week had been no exception, and with Maedchen following him he had started out punctually. Cap'n Auss Daley, our jolly neighbor, had chanced to join him and together they walked up the Ridge.

"I was a jokin' with him as we walked along," Cap'n Auss told us. "I asked him if he were afraid of ghosts down there around your place."

"'I'm not afraid of no ghosts,' he said to me. 'The only ones I've seen down there are live ones and they don't skeer me.' We walked along joking like that all the way up the West Ridge, and suddenly Parker said to me, 'I can't go on'—and fell right in my arms. I think he died almost instantly."

We were told by others that in the excitement that followed, nobody paid any attention to Maedchen, who sensed that something had happened to her beloved Parker, and finally went home alone where she howled sorrowfully throughout the night. Next morning Stella May, our neighbor, was able to persuade her to come indoors, and she was still lying in mourning under their kitchen table when we arrived home.

We stopped at the home of Parker's sister on our way to Crab's Hole. There other friends had come to pay their respect. We were ushered into the small parlor where Parker lay in his coffin, his crippled hands at rest, dressed as he had been when we took our memorable trip with him to New York. How grateful we were as we stood there by the bier of our precious Parker that we had been able to bring him our love and devotion for a brief period in his life, that we hadn't postponed those trips which meant so much to him and the memory of which would now be of equal value to us.

Death had never before struck closely in the lives of either of us; and it may sound maudlin to say that the passing of an old, crippled, uneducated man so affected us that when at last we reached the haven of our kitchen, after talking with sympathetic friends along the road, we both sat at the table and wept. There about us were poignant evidences of the presence of Parker. On the kitchen counter, stacked neatly to be washed upon his return from the barber shop, were his breakfast dishes. I rejoiced to see that he had eaten some ham and some of the blackberries he and I had picked together the summer before and which I had canned under his watchful eyes. The couch bed was made up carefully and on the table alongside was a small pile of clean underclothing and socks for the weekly Saturday change. On the bay window table lay one of the numbers of the National Geographic which he had always loved; as a marker for his place he had inserted one of his packages of cigarette papers. He had been reading the previous night—his glasses lay alongside the magazine—about the life of Eskimos. Had we been home and had we been able to have had another enjoyable tea party he would have given us, in his own delectable style, a resumé of that article. Sentimental as always, I put away the magazine with its marker in safe keeping, just as I have left his small ashtray in its own place on the kitchen window sill to remind us, should we need reminding, of those ne'er-to-be-forgotten afternoons when Parker's spirit and ours went wandering off into reminiscences of the past, and forth into the imaginative future. I discovered, too, that Parker had, even in those short days that he had enjoyed himself alone in our kitchen, found a way to help us. One of the upper kitchen cupboards had warped from the heat of the range and refused to stay tightly fastened. A small stick, smoothly carved with Parker's penknife, now was thrust through the handles of the two parts of the cupboard door, a simple but effective remedy. Henry has offered to repair that cupboard, but he knows that his offer won't be seized upon, for he knows that little stick spells Parker's thoughtfulness. Two years after Parker's death, that little stick remains in its place.

That night Henry and I joined Parker's family and friends at his home. Tangier still clings to the ancient custom of sitting up with its dead, a wearying and probably unnecessary custom, it is true, but tied up with respect, loyalty, and friendship for the departed. This was our first experience at such a gathering. As the hours crept along toward midnight, and then into the small hours of the morning, the stories of old times with which the watchers kept themselves awake grew fewer and farther apart. Those folks not closely connected with the family left for home, one by one, until only a few of Parker's nearest kinfolk, and Henry and I, remained. Finally the agony of keeping awake was too much for Henry and he, too, gave in to the flesh and left for Crab's Hole. With the greatest of effort I managed to keep my eyes open, to contribute an occasional bit of small talk, and to remain until dawn.

All funerals on Tangier are held in the church. It is custom for the near relatives to gather at the home for a few minutes before the appointed hour and to follow the coffin in solemn procession as it is carried on a wheeled stretcher over the narrow roads. Henry and I asked for permission to follow Parker's body with those who were his kin; and as the family formed in line, the closest in relationship leading, we took our place at the end, and for the last time walked with our friend across the marsh. At the close of the simple church service we went with the procession the short distance to the grave that had been prepared for Parker.

Our first thought when we heard of Parker's death was that we should like to have him buried in the small burying lot adjacent to Crab's Hole, in the old tradition of Tangier. Parker, however, had other friends besides us, and of longer duration. One of these, Cap'n Ranford Spence, with whom Parker had sailed the bay long ago, and who since has joined him in death, had offered a lot in the small graveyard belonging to his property, out of old friendship's sake. Thus it was in Cap'n Ranford's plot that we now saw Parker's body laid to rest.

Henry and I but rarely visit the grave, now marked with the plain headstone we felt Parker would want. We have no need of a marker to remind us of our friend. Parker, to us, still sits in his chair in the bay window, drinking his coffee, and smiling with happiness.

AND THERE WAS LIGHT

Now that Tangier streets are aglow with electric lights, and now that we have but to push a button again to bring the wonders of electricity into our home, it is fun already to reminisce about the three-and-a-half years when we lived in comparative darkness. Those years were an experience that I would not have lifted from my life. When I open the kitchen cupboard and glance at the row of kerosene lamps on the top shelf, filled in readiness for the day when a storm may temporarily put the electric plant out of commission, I am conscious of a feeling of tenderness for them as for old-and-true companions.

At any rate I am willing to forget the tedious daily task that was mine to fill the lamps and trim the wicks and polish the chimneys. When we first came to Tangier I could never seem to remember this job until dusk, when it was time to light the lamps. Filled they could be at the last minute, but I discovered early that glass chimneys could not be tardily washed since they would crack before completely dry. Day after day I would do a makeshift job with a piece of tissue paper, feeling guiltily envious of the shining lamps of my neighbors. At last I hit upon a solution for my forgetfulness. Efficiently, I had arranged a place for my lamps on a shelf inside the big kitchen closet where they were hidden from my sight. Now the remembrance came to me of the mantel in my grandmother's home, where in view of all she kept her row of pink, blue, green, and white glass lamps. Ours were not pretty, or made of lovely hob-nail glass as were hers, but nevertheless I decided that they should be placed daily on a little table beneath the kitchen clock, in full view. Thereafter I needed but one morning caller to catch me with my lamp chimneys blackened, and the oil in the lamps unreplenished, for me to reform my ways.

The task of caring for the lamps eventually became a matter of pride, too. The morning dishes were washed and dried as quickly as possible; and then, with plenty of piping hot water and soap, the chimneys were sozzled and resozzled in the suds, rinsed quickly, and polished with cloths made from old feed bags—which, Miss Nora informed me, left the least amount of lint and made the glass sparkle.

When I first began to trim the wicks of the lamps I was reminded of the woman who, in an effort to straighten the line of her lawn hedge, trimmed and trimmed until the hedge disappeared. The art of making a slick, clean slash at the carbon came after much trial and error. Then there was the oil to be considered. With reckless speed I invariably poured too much into the funnel, and the overflow added a smelly and unnecessary task to my labors. Parker's natural efficiency came to my rescue after a morning when the breakfast toast tasted suspiciously of kerosene. His procedure involved newspapers, used later for the fireplace, plus a slow, patient pouring of the oil.

The reward of all this came at twilight when I could smirk with pride as Henry lit the evening lamps which now sent out their straight, steady flame within their shining chimneys, giving to our supper table a soft and happy glow. I recall with special affection our first winter at Tangier, when Sylvia, Owen, and Mark were all attending school on the island (Kent was off in the Army), when I was doing substitute teaching, and Henry was already exploring the possibilities of a project to create a new power plant. On the cold, dark, windy evenings of January and February the only room we could properly heat in our house was its large kitchen-dining room. With all the lamps in the house collected in the middle of the dining table, the children gathered around and did their homework, I did my class preparations, and Henry worked on his extensive correspondence. The cats would curl up on the sofa, and Maedchen slept under the table. For a couple of hours the family rule was, minimum conversation.

All this togetherness in the magical embrace of the light and the warmth from our assembled kerosene lamps! Indeed, those were moments that none of us in our family would ever lift from our lives.

When we first came to Tangier the town did, in fact, have an antiquated electric plant which produced direct current. Tottering with age, it was unable to work full time; and so the electricity was turned on about five o'clock in the afternoon, then switched off again rather promptly at 10:30. Because of the low voltage and the direct current, which necessitated special equipment, only a small percentage of the islanders had their homes linked to these power lines. Electricity not being available during the morning and afternoon, washing machines and electric irons were impracticable, while electric refrigeration was of course out of the question. The wires were strung on low poles, and in many stretches the insulation hung loose from the wires in strips that dangled in the breeze. The poles had not been set very deep, and during every storm several of them would predictably fall across the narrow streets. When the old engine gasped its last, about a year after our arrival, there were few tears shed. Missed most of all were the street lights, which though few in number and very dim, did help a bit to make walking safer at night.

Henry was aware of the important work which had been accomplished by the Rural Electrification Administration. The REA had been founded back in 1935, its specific mission being to bring electricity to communities so remote that they could not be serviced profitably by private companies. Realizing that Tangier Island was precisely the sort of community that this agency had been created to benefit, Henry early had the dream to bring Tangier to the attention of the REA. Having been elected a member of the town council, he found the other members equally anxious to see Tangier equipped with a modern plant, and so an appeal was made to Washington. Representatives of the REA made an initial survey; but, to our chagrin, they reported that Tangier's population was not sufficiently large to warrant the construction of an electric plant here. And, they further reported, it would be entirely too expensive to connect the island with mainland plants by means of a cable. Hence, there seemed but one solution: to construct a town-owned plant, and either to supplement its cost of maintenance by money-raising schemes, or to charge a very high rate for electric consumption. The town was too poor to take on the burden of borrowing the amount needed, and so the council asked for contributions to a newly created "Electric Fund" in the form of shares, to be paid back with interest later on.

The watermen of the island at this time were more prosperous than they had been in many years, due to wartime prices for seafood; but they remembered all too well the hard days of the Depression, and so were reluctant to part with their money for what seemed to many a reckless and crazy plan. Some argued that their money would be lost, as it had been in several unfortunate business ventures attempted on the island in earlier years. Others voiced the opinion that they had done without electricity all their lives, and could continue to do so. There were, as always, some few with vision and with faith—and the contributions of these people were sufficient to enable the council to proceed with the installation of poles and lines, and with the construction of a small building to be used as an office, and to house two electric generators, obtained from government war-surplus stock. Then in December, 1946, the council came up against a stone wall. Transformers, ordered several months before, were still unavailable. We ourselves sent pleading letters to everyone we could learn about who was in any way connected with the manufacture of transformers—but to no avail.

Hope soared briefly at one point when it looked as if we might be getting the transformers because someone on the island knew someone who knew someone else who was in a position to obtain them—but this turned out to be just a pipe dream. And so the weeks went by...with the engines still silent. Those who refused to subscribe to the "Electric Fund" said, "I told you so!" with a certain private glee; and even those who had subscribed began to feel resigned to the loss of their money, so small was their faith.

Henry and I spent a couple of months that winter in Williamsburg. While we were there the REA held its annual convention in Richmond, and Henry decided to attend it, entertaining the faint hope that some of the REA electric cooperatives might just have some extra transformers which they could lend us until our order came through from the manufacturer. This hope was quickly eliminated. Still, as a result of that trip, undertaken on the spur of the moment, came electricity for Tangier Island.

Soon after the convention Henry and I returned to Tangier, stopping off enroute at Norfolk, at an electrical supply house, to check the chances of getting those transformers. Our errand to Norfolk was mentioned in a letter sent ahead to a friend on Tangier. Our friend told another person casually that we were trying to see what could be done about the transformers; that person told another...and so it went until the story finally reached this version: we had been successful in obtaining those essential transformers, and were bringing them back to the island with us. We thought an unusual crowd awaited us at the Tangier wharf, but were unprepared for the question, "Where are the transformers?"...and the downcast look on the faces of the people when they learned that this rumor which had so aroused their hopes was false.

Early in the spring, however, came a blessed letter from the REA, saying that Henry's earnest plea for transformers, and his picture of the seriousness of our situation, had, in fact, spurred several of the engineers to make a further study of our island's need. By chance they had discovered that Smith Island, our neighbor to the north, had made a similar request for REA assistance some years before—and had likewise been turned down. Now it seemed to the engineers that a combination of the two islands—thus doubling the number of potential consumers—might be feasible. The letter informed us that preliminary studies had been made that looked hopeful, and spoke of the imminent visit to the island of a team of REA representatives. They came, they approved—and, in the best attended town meeting we had ever been able to produce, the now enthusiastic team from the REA convinced the islanders.

To shorten a long tale, the town sold its plant and equipment to the REA, and there was created "The Chesapeake Islands Electric Cooperative." From this new enterprise, just before Christmas of 1947, electricity was generated for Tangier Island.

At this moment Smith Island is still without lights, since the work of building the overhead pole lines across the many little marshy islands that string between Tangier and our neighbor to the north is not yet completed. This has been a long and tedious job, depending for its progress on the whims of wind and tide. Nearly all of the homes on Smith Island—"Smith's Island," as it's called on Tangier—have been wired in readiness, and before long they, too, will be enjoying the benefits of electric power. Smith islanders (who are Marylanders) and Tangiermen (who are Virginians) have, alas, not always been the best of friends over the years. Feuds over crabbing grounds and oyster beds have at times been bitter. Therefore, not the least of the gains to be derived from our electric cooperative has been the new spirit of friendship and trust that has been nurtured between the two communities.

Last May on Tangier we celebrated the first anniversary of the founding of The Chesapeake Islands Electric Cooperative. Though the night was stormy, a large group of Smith islanders braved the choppy sound to attend the meeting in our hall of The Daughters of America which was packed to the window sills. Prizes of electric toasters and fans were given away to lucky-number holders, an REA documentary film was shown, Tangier and Smith islanders shared in a talent show, and of course ice cream and cake were consumed in quantity. Jean and Jess Ogden of the Extension Bureau of the University of Virginia were in attendance, and Professor Ogden made the principal speech of the evening. The Ogdens have since written a splendid account of what electricity has done for our island, in the June 1948 issue of their New Dominion series, published in Charlottesville, Virginia.

They write, "The islanders are quiet and cautious in their expressions of enthusiasm. Yet there was apparent in their response to this first annual meeting a sense of pride and self-confidence. It was a very different response, the Mayor said, from that of the first meeting called by the town council, to consider the original plan of a town electric plant. About thirty had responded to that initial call, and their attitude was largely one of skepticism. Now, however, they have convinced themselves by their own achievement that they can do whatever they want to do, if they plan and work together."

Electricity has indeed been joyfully received on Tangier Island! As it began to look more and more certain that power would actually be sent through those wires that had been strung (but remained so long unused), and after the shareholders in the original venture had received checks for their shares—plus interest—one by one the objectors became silent. When finally the power switch was turned on, all were loud in their requests to have their homes wired for electricity.

Oh yes, there were still criticisms—new criticisms. Some said the streets were now too brightly lit. One woman complained that her electric iron was much too hot. I myself had become so unaccustomed to electric appliances that I likewise burned my fingers on the toaster and the waffle iron—and so added my own complaints to the others, facetiously. Luckily the arrival of electricity on the island coincided with the appearance on the market of more and more appliances—after long years of war-time shortages. Nowadays, when the mail boat arrives each afternoon it has become a common sight to see washing machines, refrigerators, and electric stoves being lifted to the dock. Two of the town's stores have become agencies for well-known appliance manufacturers. And now, we note, a common pest of the mainland has appeared on Tangier, in the form of the vacuum-cleaner salesman, who has found our island to be fertile soil for his sales-talk.

We in our family, in all our years before we came to Tangier, had been so accustomed to the modern conveniences that go along with electricity that we never imagined the possibility of being thrilled by such things. Now, however, again and again as we touch a switch we are indeed thrilled—and take joy in our appreciation of how our lives have been changed. It is such fun to watch the vacuum cleaner sucking up all that sand that is forever being tracked into our house. We have revived one of our favorite family rituals from Connecticut days: the Sunday night supper of waffles. We understand the amusing "complaint" of one neighbor, that since the coming of electricity her bread bill had soared, since her family wanted toast at every meal, just for the fun of watching the bread pop up out of the toaster.

An electric hot water heater makes it possible for us to have hot showers at other times than midwinter, when the kitchen range could heat the water tank. Along with this pleasure, however, is lost another: that of sneaking three baths a day—when we're on the mainland, and have access to a modern bathroom.

Best of all is the refrigerator! Before the arrival of electricity it was usual that we bought blocks of ice three or four times a week. We were compelled to when we had the cows, to prevent the milk from souring. But then there was the usual concern for preserving other foods—and the special concern of having lots of ice for iced tea during the long humid months of the summer. When Parker was with us he made the frequent long journeys to the dock in his skiff, provided there was a sufficiently high tide. Should the boys and Henry not be on hand when Parker returned, he and I worked out a method of getting the ice into the chest without too much strain. His crippled hands weren't strong enough to heft the hundred-pound cake (often reduced, however, to about seventy-five pounds from the summer sun), so we arranged a skid which usually worked excellently; but when on occasion the ice slipped off, we were just out of luck, and had to wait for the return of one of the members of the family equipped with brawn. After Parker's death the whole task fell to whichever boy was available, and he would need to use a wheelbarrow for the mile-long push to carry ice from the dock down to Crab's Hole.

When news of our purchase of a new electric refrigerator reached Owen at college, he wrote back, "The first thing I shall do upon reaching home is to make a bee-line to the refrigerator and make myself a glass of iced tea with ice that I haven't had to push through the heat of the sun!"

This past summer's consumption of ice cubes would indeed be difficult to record; and we still haven't become so accustomed to this luxury but that we often remark on how wonderful it is to be able to use all the ice we want!

Another exquisite transformation in our lives these days is that we now have an electric phonograph. (These past four years we could only play records on a wind-up Victrola—though that never held Owen back!) Of late Henry and I have been taking time to explore the family record collection, which was mostly built up by our music-loving middle-son. Just recently I had occasion to attend an evening meeting up in the town; and as I returned home and crossed the bridge leading to Crab's Hole, I noticed that all the lights in the house were out—the electric lights, that is. The living room, on the other hand, was lit by the glow of candles. Entering the house, I discovered my music-loving husband, all by himself, lost in his contemplation of the slow movement of the Beethoven Violin Concerto.

Progress, once started, has a way of keeping on; and so it will be on Tangier. Now that electricity is here, the possibility of having a town water system is in the early talking stages. With electric power now available to pump water into a storage tank, artesian wells, drilled to a depth below the floor of the Chesapeake Bay, could bring an ample supply of water, and so replace the present unsanitary surface wells, which are few and far between on this island, and the rain-water storage tanks, such as we depend on down at Crab's Hole. The town council, in its new drive for a town water system, hopes that it will now have greater backing and faith from the Tangier folk, who have learned, as the Odgens mention in their report, some of the rewards and joys of working together. To those of us who long to see this island come into its own, further developments are now ahead as a result of the coming of electricity.

THE RETURN
OF THE NATIVES

M OST OF THE TANGIER BOYS (and young women, as well) who went off to the war, came back to live the rest of their lives, they hoped, on the island. Similarly, several families that went away to work in defense factories have returned to their old homes. On the other hand we note that during the past the Tangier community has lost occasional members to the mainland. A few island girls have married men from other localities and have departed permanently, while other boys and girls have gone away to college and have found positions elsewhere. So strong has been the tie that has bound the sons and daughters of Tangier to their former home, however, that a number of years ago the Methodist church established here the institution of Homecoming—and this wonderful annual event has steadily grown in popularity. No former Tangierman who can possibly manage the trip will neglect to return to his birthplace each year for this special August celebration.

While the proceeds of earlier Homecomings went to the church treasury—which in Depression days sorely needed the assistance—

the primary purpose of this event was social. The celebrations were held on the long strip of beach that separated the harbor of Tangier from the Bay. On the important day many boatloads of people crowded the sandbar, and long hours were spent in conversation about old times and in the relating of all the news that concerned the wanderers from home, as well as the island folk themselves. Enormous quantities of food were consumed at the temporary food counters which the town fathers erected over on the beach for this happy occasion.

When crabs and oysters came into their own during the war years and brought good prices to the watermen, prosperity came likewise to the church treasury. Thus, when the town council was carrying on its drive for funds for the new electric plant, the church consented that the town should itself take charge of the annual Homecoming. With more emphasis on the money-raising possibilities of the celebration, the location of the Homecoming festivities was transferred from the beach (whose contours were altered considerably by storms and by shifting winds a few years ago) to a vacant lot near the docks. With the extension of Homecoming to two days, then to three days, this event has turned into Tangier Island's most exciting holiday of the year. Each succeeding year sees an ever increasing crowd descending upon the island during the first week of August. The hostess of the Chesapeake Inn, the town's only hostelry, is swamped with reservations in advance. All the housewives are busy for days ahead, not only getting their own homes highly polished for homecoming relatives, but cooking food for the Homecoming booths as well. Fences that weren't whitewashed or painted in the spring are hastily put into shape. Unkempt lawns are neatly cut. Flowers are placed on the graves of relatives. Everyone gets spruced up for the occasion. Children stop spending money at the stores, and competition runs high in the race to save up for the spending spree ahead.

Henry and I have worked on the Homecoming committee in one capacity or another for the past three years. This experience has taught us and our fellow workers that there are several essentials in the Homecoming as it has now evolved. The first, of course, is FOOD—and plenty of it! Sandwiches of all sorts, soft drinks, and ice cream are the favorite items, and are served from a large refreshment booth which occupies the center of the Homecoming grounds. In addition it was necessary this past summer to serve dinners in the hall of The Daughters of America, especially for out-of-town guests who come in on the excursion boats that run from the Eastern and Western Shores. Hundreds of soft crabs, gallons of ground clams made into fritters, and countless hotdogs and hamburgers were consumed by the crowds at the last Homecoming. I remember well one sad-faced little boy who stood near me on the last night, as he was spending his final pennies for one of the few remaining hotdogs.

"Gee," he mourned, "I wisht Homecomin' was startin' all over agin tomorrow. This is my twelfth hotdog today!"

Soft drinks, always popular on Tangier, disappeared as fast as the money in the folks' pockets. Long after people had tired of the games on the grounds, and the entertainment provided on the speaker's platform, they clung to the counters and ate, while the weary women whose shift it was to serve up the sandwiches, and the boys who jerked the caps off the Coca-Cola bottles, prayed for their departure. Were statistics taken of the stomachaches that occur on the island after each Homecoming they could tell the tale of what this is all about. But, like the pains of childbirth, the discomfort that comes from overeating is soon forgotten; and each August finds the townsfolk ready for another Big Time.

When three years ago Homer Williams strung lights from his Delco generator to brighten the Homecoming lot, and then installed a loudspeaker system on the speaker's platform, he initiated a new requirement for a proper Tangier Homecoming: lots of noise. Whether the noise is that of jazz records blaring forth to assault the ears of the most distant islander, or the singing of local talent, the townspeople have come to like a lot of loud music to support the excitement of their Homecoming.

Speakers from the Eastern Shore, town boys who have "made

good" in the outside world, are urged to step to the microphone. Even Virginia's Governor Tuck once favored the island with a visit to our Homecoming; and when he gave a speech he received the "shoutin'-est" reception in memory.

Every year, as a main attraction for Homecoming, the town's baseball team sets up a match with a team from the mainland, or from neighboring Smith Island. The young people of the island would be pleased were there a game each day of the Homecoming festival; but the committee decided this past year that since our only baseball diamond was a bit distant from the food booths, too many ballgames would detract from the sales of soft crabs and hamburgers. Hence, the town's ball-fans were obliged to condense their shouting energy into the hours of a single exciting afternoon.

The people of Tangier Island have long had a truly amazing repertory of traditional gospel hymns. Returning kinsmen, most of them hungry for such music from their childhood days, enjoy more than anything else at Homecoming the evening devoted to an outdoor old-time hymn-sing. It has occurred to us that vacation schooners which include Tangier Island in their Chesapeake Bay cruises during the summer months might well plan to put into harbor on the evening of such a Homecoming hymn-sing. Listening to "Abide With Me" coming across the Tangier harbor on a moonlit night, sung by hundreds and hundreds of Tangier voices, young and old, on the occasion of their reunion with their homecoming friends and relatives, would be a moment never to be forgotten.

The final requirement for a perfect Homecoming is some means by which the children might, quite literally, be taken for a ride. The first year that Homecoming was held on the Main Ridge it was my thought to bring onto the island a Jeep for just this purpose. With no automobiles on the island, all forms of land-traveling motor vehicles are all but unknown to the children here, and so a ride on a Jeep was bound to be a hit with the kids. Through the aid of Mr. West, our county commissioner, contact was made with the naval base at Chincoteague Island; and an "exhibition" Jeep, in charge of a most cheerful navy officer, was generously lent to

Tangier to help out with our Homecoming.

The poor officer's two-day stay on the island was as busy as any he'd known in peacetime service, it is certain. Children of all ages swarmed over the Jeep, and at ten cents a ride a tidy sum was added to our fund for a new electric plant. As the officer made his very slow rides along the Main Ridge to transport some of the elderly ladies to the fairground it became necessary to forbid the town's children from climbing onto his little Jeep. For everyone on Tangier not only was this their first such experience on the island, for some members of our community this was the very first time they had ever ridden in any kind of a "car." That summer elderly people were again and again driven up and down on the Main Ridge, an experience they would never forget. The navy officer also reported it was an experience he, too, would never forget.

The next year we brought to the island's Homecoming our ancient Buick—which had just returned from taking our family on a camping trip to the West Coast. (By this point the old wreck had gone almost 200,000 miles!) Kent and I took turns maneuvering this old car through the narrow turn of the street near the Church, and slowly down the three-quarter-mile stretch of the Main Ridge, where at the very end, with several backings, we were able to turn the thing around—thanks to some helpful folks who had a yard without a picket fence. We finally gave up all efforts to keep children off the fenders, and quietly prayed that none would get hurt. The deliberately slow speed of our "progress" made the likelihood of any injuries quite remote; still, at the end of those three days our nerves were in a jittery state. When we returned the old Buick to its parking lot in Crisfield, we swore that never again would we bring a car on the island—where cars just have no place.

At the most recent Homecoming we didn't have to search for a vehicle. The town council had just purchased a "town tractor" —with a little trailer. The trailer held plenty of children when packed in, sardine-like, by the driver, Jack McCready. The tractor did double duty, functioning as a money-maker through the rides that it provided for the children, and as a labor-lightener, by assisting in the hauling of soft drinks, ice, tables and chairs, and all the other paraphernalia required for a successful Homecoming.

When the last hour of the last night was at hand, when the last penny had been counted by the committee in charge, and when I discovered that my poor aching feet couldn't possibly carry me the long walk to Crab's Hole, the tractor came to my rescue, In the company of the last youthful stragglers who were still hanging on, lest a single moment of fun be lost, Henry and I enjoyed a rough but welcome ride down the Main Ridge, across the marsh road, and as far down the lane to Crab's Hole as the narrowing path would permit. Like its predecessors, the Jeep and the old Buick, the town tractor took its place as a giver of joy for the Tangier Homecoming.

THIS WAY AND THAT

T ANGIER ISLAND has long been a target for newspaper reporters. An unsolved murder, the mischievous and disorderly pranks of restless youth—such things are common enough happenings all over the country, but take on an added interest when reported from an island. Journalists have reported tales of the clannishness of the Tangier people and have shown pictures of their homes and of their narrow streets, with certainly no intention of being unkind. Occasionally, however, items have been included that have seemed to the island folk to infer ridicule. The result has been a strong antagonism for all publicity, which is unfortunate, since the people have in their customs and manners here, and in the strange beauty of their town, a unique way of life of which they can be rightly proud.

First of all, we residents of the island should proclaim afar our freedom from the noise of the automobile. The only encroachments of modern transportation on Tangier's streets are the town tractor and a few motor-driven scooters. An automobile can pass with difficulty along the main street, can turn only at the very end of the mile-long road, but, of course, cannot possibly pass another car.

Hence, its usefulness here is minimal. The town tractor has already been put to good use in the transportation of coal and other heavy loads, and may eventually be the means of a program of garbage collection—at present an acute problem on the island both from the standpoint of the town's beauty and of its sanitation. But the whir of automobile motors, the screeching of brakes, and the accompanying danger that automobiles produce for pedestrians are lacking on Tangier, and this very lack is one of our greatest blessings. True, there are disadvantages in having to attend a meeting on foot on a very rainy night, but we Tangiermen solve that problem simply enough by remaining at home. After all, there is always another night for the meeting. The enforced walking which people on the West Ridge in particular must do gives us all a better appetite and helps us to keep down our avoirdupois.

Newspapers write of the custom which Tangier women have of wearing bonnets for at least nine months of the year. Young teenage girls have thrown off this habit, having caught some of the fever for a stylish tan; but most of them when they are once married return to the ways of the older women. Having spent several summers in the hot wind that sweeps the island I must admit the wisdom of wearing bonnets and wish that I could overcome my dislike for anything whatsoever on my head in the summertime in order to save my skin from the heavy beating it takes each year. It is a pleasant picture to see the sun-bonneted women chatting over their picket fences; and far from being embarrassed by this custom, the people should cling to it as a picturesque and most sensible habit.

Years ago there were very few people living on the island, and so each family owned considerable land. Rather than carry their dead to the mainland—often a physical impossibility—they buried their kin in small family graveyards discreetly distanced from their homes, but within the embrace of the family property. As the island's population grew, and unused land became scarce, homes gradually were built in closer and closer proximity to the graveyards, and the newer graves were often placed in the very dooryard. With a smaller population this did not involve any health problem, and it did enable the townsfolk to honor the graves of their loved ones with great care and to visit them, which would have been difficult were the burials to be made on the mainland. Finally, the town's population became so much greater that plots of land were set apart for public cemeteries; and instead of direct burial in the ground, the bodies were placed in cement vaults, the upper six inches or so being above ground. These vaults are kept neatly painted; and at Easter, Christmas, Mother's Day, Homecoming, or family anniversaries, family graves on Tangier Island are lovingly decorated with flowers. The time is inevitably not far off, however, when burial on the island will no longer be possible. On the other hand, with the fast engines of the modern motorboat the difficulties that faced the early residents will not be present.

Naturally, to people from the mainland, where land is without limit, the presence of gravestones in a small front yard is strange. Often reporters have attempted to take pictures of the dooryard gravestones, without first obtaining permission. Sometimes they have met with vehement disapproval. Greater tact on the part of visitors from outside, combined with the growth of local pride in a tradition of historical interest (plus perhaps a development of the sense of humor of the Tangier folk) will all help to dispel the sometimes unpleasant suspicion that exists toward the transient tourist to the island. While living here, we have tried to persuade our neighbors and friends that it is the difference in customs the world over that makes travel interesting. Should every one of our ancestors have had exactly the same way of doing everything under the sun, it would indeed be now a monotonous old planet. I am sure that someday we who live on Tangier will gladly display our little dooryard gravestones to the traveler as reminders of those days and those customs that have gone forever. Crab's Hole has its own small graveyard with five headstones which we tend as carefully as were they our own ancestors who lie there; and we are proud of the snapshots sent us recently by some tourists who asked permission to photograph this place that has come to mean so much to us.

On New Year's morning on Tangier Island there is an early

knock at everyone's door. On the doorstep will be one or more small boys who will enter with the query, "New Year's Gift?" Clinging to the ancient superstition—whose origin I have been unable to ascertain—that it is bad luck if the first visitor of the year to cross the threshold is female, but good luck if that visitor be male, the people continue to welcome the early visits of the town's small boys, crossing their outstretched little hands with silver. Assembling in the streets later in the day the boys boast of their day's pickings, and I am sure that it will be a long time before this ancient custom is discarded if the Tangier lads have anything to say about it.

Much has been made in published articles of the remnants of old Elizabethan speech in the language of the Tangier community. Not having any knowledge of early language I am unable to judge to what extent this is true, but even to the unpracticed ear there are certain words and phrases that appear in the speech of the older people (though these are gradually disappearing), and certain vowel pronunciations that are certainly of early English origin. Parker's speech was packed with unusual words, and I wished after his death that I had written them down more faithfully. He spoke so often of being "sob wet"—an expression that mystified me, until I found it listed in our Merriam-Webster Unabridged Dictionary among English expressions now obsolete. Parker frequently used the word "we're" for "our": as in "We were getting we're boats tied up." He would go to the dentist to have a tooth pulled, he assured me, after the swelling had "suaged"—which I found to be the obsolete dialectic English form of "assuaged". He called the small seat in a rowboat a "thaught", which likewise I found to be the old form of "thwart", the nautical term for such a seat. For a long time I thought that the common pronunciation "drudge", for the harrowing of the ocean beds for crabs and oysters, was merely a mispronunciation, and that the Tangiermen had used it to indicate the labor involved. This I also found to be the obsolete and dialectic form of "dredge". I once heard a Tangier woman say that her father was "a great hand to prog". "Prog" is a very old word indeed, and originally meant "to pick up a living by begging or thieving". As used on Tangier the word came to mean "picking up clams or oysters, or catching some fish when food supplies were low".

Parker always spoke of "neighbors" as though the word were spelled "nibors"—with a long "i"—and of the "niles" he was hammering, and of the "siles" of a boat. Then at times he would say, "What ails ('iles') that?", meaning, we came to learn, "Isn't that strange, though?" This pronunciation of the long "a" vowel sound is standard on Tangier Island, for old and young—just as to this day it remains standard on the British Isles among people of the working classes.

Henry, in working with his young carpenter apprentices on the island, has had fun joking with them about the "niles" which they are using—and equally amused when they retaliate by mocking his habit of sticking an "r" into his pronunciation of "oil"—a hangover from his boyhood days in Brooklyn. Amused and glad he is, too, that they are so aware of the fact that Tangier is a place unto itself, with its own delicious spin on the English language.

The short sound of the vowel "a" is likewise somewhat changed by the Tangier tongue. To the little children who shout their greetings as we go along the path to Crab's Hole we are not Mr. and Mrs. "Jander", but Mr. and Mrs. "Jiander". When they have a scrap with one another they are "miad"; and when they do something wrong they are "biad" boys.

For the long double "ee", such as occurs in "feed" or "see", Tangier English has a sound something akin to the German umlaut—yet not really the same. One has to come to Tangier Island to hear this special sound.

In the musical inflection of the voice there is a similarity between these people and the Welsh people among whom I was raised. Always their voices rise at the end of a sentence; and even in the simple expression, "Well!"—to express surprise or disgust—the word is left curling in the air, rather than pushed to the earth, as others pronounce it.

One of the most interesting customs of speech on the island is what they themselves call "talking over-the-left." This consists of saying, in even the simplest remarks, the exact opposite of the meaning intended. Just as it is not unusual for people elsewhere to say, "Well, this is a nice day!"—on a very rainy morning—Tangier folk will employ this speech mannerism at all times. If I wear a pretty dress for the first time, a child will say to me, "That's a poor dress"; or should it be raining pitchforks he will comment, "It ain't rainin' none." Only by the subtle tone of voice can one ascertain the true meaning; and after almost five years of residence on Tangier I still occasionally confuse the message.

Substituting in the high school the first winter after we moved here, I had numerous embarrassing experiences, until I learned to recognize whether the pupils were answering normally, or speaking "over the left". "That's an easy lesson" meant it was an extremely difficult one. "Yes" often meant "No".

Older people on the island, when they play this trick of language, will often say something like this: "I had a poor visit—over the left." The younger people, however, are so familiar with this habit that they find no need for the old signal. Inquiring among the Tangier folk for the origin of this custom, I failed completely to trace it. People of the age of sixty or younger claim that they cannot remember when the custom hadn't existed. Folks of seventy-five or so insist that they did not use it as small children.

I think that perhaps I have found, by accident, the mystery of the "over-the-left" twist in Tangier English. One day I was visiting a historic home in Richmond, and fell into conversation with the curator of the place, a woman of some sixty-odd years. Telling her about the island and some of its delightful customs, I chanced to mention "over-the-left" speech, and stated that I had been unable to find out how it began. She recalled that when she was a child in the town of Petersburg on the James River, this usage was common among the young people there. A form of slang, she considered it. Like other slang expressions it had its day, as she recollected, and then passed from the speech of the people in that region. We both decided that perhaps Tangier watermen, fishing or oystering in the James River, had acquired this usage and brought it home to the island. For some unknown reason—perhaps a desire to conceal their true thoughts from prying strangers=the people of Tangier cherished the custom, and made it a part of their everyday language.

Because the social life of the men and women here is quite separated, there is a certain shyness about any public demonstration of affection between husband and wife. When Henry and I walk down the street arm in arm, we are still met with amusement, often expressed aloud.

"You two are like dories tied to a barge," laughed Miss Nora once, as she met us. Others remarked, "Here come the old sweethearts"—with laughter, but no ridicule in their voices.

Some of the other customs on Tangier are simply the same ones that exist all over the country in rural communities. Men here congregate in the early evening in the store to discuss the day's catch, and to share the latest gossip. Young people take their "dates" to church, and sit in the very back pews, listening not a whit to the sermon, but slyly holding hands when nobody is looking. These are not customs indigenous to Tangier Island, but they do add their share to giving to this town its quality of other-world-ness.

I remember well when the Tangier council was first beginning its efforts to bring electricity to the island, that a message was sent to us, via our daughter, from a woman on the Eastern Shore, begging us to have no part in the "modernization" of Tangier.

"Do let the island stay just as it always was. Don't bring modern conveniences to the town!"

I wondered whether this woman were herself compelled to carry eighteen or twenty pails of water the distance of a couple of city blocks in order to do the family wash, working over a scrub-board, and were she unable to enjoy electric refrigeration, or the convenience of good lighting, she would then be so anxious to keep the town "just as it always was."

It doesn't matter, however, whether some people wish to hold on to the old just because it is old. The advent of modern conveniences in isolated communities is inevitable. Through the movies, and over the radio, people learn of the ways by which folk elsewhere lighten their daily tasks. With that awareness they will not rest contented—nor should they rest contented—until they have their share of the good things in life. The men and women on Tangier Island have as much right to be able to live comfortably as have the people in any community.

In their ability to push a button to get electricity, or to turn on a faucet to get water, they need sacrifice none of the truly important things that make Tangier a delightfully unique community. Because of the narrowness of the island's ridges, and the preciousness of every inch of space, our town will surely never widen its streets and become a community with automobiles—with all that would be lost, should that happen. With automobiles, Tangier would sacrifice its beauty as the very special island it now is.

Due to the houses being so close to one another, picket fences will always be needed here to maintain a sense of privacy. And there is nothing that lends such charm to a street than does a row of picket fences.

The historic gravestones are there, and, with pride in their care, will remain to show the customs of by-gone days.

There will always be hot winds sweeping the island; and if the women remain wise, they will cling to their protective sunbonnets.

Speech, however, is something over which no man has control; and since speech is constantly changing everywhere in the world, it will very likely also change here on this protected island.

In the meantime it is our hope that the Tangier people will move into a future where their lives are better, yet where they continue to take pride in the unique beauty of their past.

MUD BETWEEN OUR TOES

A RECENT ISSUE of Life magazine contained brief resumés of the experiences of some eight couples who had "escaped" from city life to the country. In a later issue one of the letters to the editors, written by a Mr. Baird Hall of Waitsfield, Vermont, pointed out that these people had made a decision that was almost the reverse of escape. They felt, he said, "the urge to come to grips with responsibilities—economic, social, political, and philosophical." At the time of our move to Tangier there were those who hinted that perhaps our venture was simply an escape from responsibility. This now seems very funny to us, for had there been even the slightest thought of "escape" in our plans—and we don't like to admit that there was—the responsibilities that we left behind now seem so materialistic, and so commonplace, compared to those we have taken on since coming to Tangier. Though at that time we would have been somewhat embarrassed to have confessed that we hoped to lead a more useful life on Tangier than we had been living in Connecticut—and though we would have been the last to proclaim that we were driven by any such mighty urge as Mr. Hall suggests—it is in fact true that the words of Cap'n Pete's wife, Miss Rose, had a considerable influence on our decision.

"We think that you folks would be a help to the island if you came here to live."

Now that sufficient time has elapsed for any evidences of our influence to have become manifest, a completely honest facing of the facts would probably reveal that most of our hopes in that direction have been in vain. Henry can undoubtedly be safe in assuming a certain credit for the accomplishment of the electrification project. He could not have accomplished it single-handed, to be sure, and the assistance of his fellow council members was indispensable; but his ability to organize, and his perseverance, were at least helpful. I think, too, Henry would like to pat himself on the back for having brought the tax lists of the town into something approaching order. Because of the similarity of names on the island, and because of the failure of past generations to record their property deeds at the county courthouse, a tremendous mix-up had developed over the years; and only weeks of tireless work on his part, involving much questioning of the older inhabitants of the town and the postmaster, whose work makes him familiar with names of the people, plus much checking of old records, and innumerable visits to Accomac, the county seat, brought any kind of order to this chaos. As a builder, too, Henry has had opportunity to be of assistance to the islanders at times. Certainly, the appearance of built-in kitchen cupboards in the houses of some of the people can be traced to the interest provoked by those that were installed in the kitchen of Crab's Hole. As for my own influence, except for the fact that a few children can now play the piano a little, and several groups of high school youngsters have seen New York on pilgrimages I've conducted to the Big City, the horrible truth is that I've had none—unless the fact that a number of women who formerly never drank hot tea, but have acquired the habit through association with me, can be considered an accomplishment.

However, if our life here among our Tangier friends hasn't resulted in the "good" that Miss Rose so optimistically imagined it would, it certainly has been worthwhile for us. This statement is made in spite of the facts that when I substituted in the high school here for a year I lost seventeen pounds which I couldn't well spare, and that recently a physical checkup showed that Henry, now in the years of middle age, will do well to rest more than we have in the past. True, we have both worked harder physically on the island than we ever did in our New England home. But the missing seventeen pounds were regained in short order at Crab's Hole where the daily rest I needed was interrupted by no phone calls nor by salesmen ringing the doorbell.

Because of living on the island we were able to take nine glorious weeks for a western camping trip with our children in a recent summer, a feat that would have defied accomplishment when Henry was in the building business in New York. And now that my husband and I must take life more easily we are planning already on another such trip, this time for just the two of us. It will mean wearing the old clothes a little longer and scrimping a speck more here and there, but we shall go!

All that, however, is but the physical side. What really matters is not whether we are a little thinner or a little weary at times but that we have learned so much here. We know that big things don't happen overnight. We came here with enthusiasm and optimism to spare, certain that the school on Tangier could be brought to the standard of the best rural schools of the nation within a few months at the most. We saw the need for electricity and for running water, for a library, for better recreational facilities for the youth of the island, for a medical and dental clinic, for better adult education. To date there is electricity on the island, and now there is talk of running water in the not-too-distant future; and a library, after four years of persistent effort, is in the final throes of birth. A parents' organization is working on the creation of a playground for the children. These few improvements have taken the combined efforts of the council, the church, and the school for several years. The other hopes we nurtured so happily are a long way yet from accomplishment, but we ourselves have learned to be patient.

Along the way, too, we have lost all the false pride we ever had. Had the disappointments we encountered through the months been insufficient to erase it, the numerous strange tales about us—mostly critical—which reached our ears would have completed the job. These tales, many of them false, most of them unkind, but a few of them well founded, not only destroyed our foolish pride but also much of the sensitiveness from which both of us had been previously unaware that we suffered. Dick Elliott, one-time pastor of the church we attended in Connecticut, and a person we were blessed to count among our friends, use to say that sensitiveness was truly but selfishness. Here on Tangier, where every word we have spoken and every move we have made have been well hashed over, we have come to know the truth of Dick Elliott's words. A polite veneer of culture which we had acquired in our earlier life had prevented us from ever relating to others the stories we may have heard about them—and likewise protected us, if such can be called protection, from knowing what was said behind our backs. No such veneer exists on Tangier; sooner or later every bit of gossip about us was repeated to us, to our discomfiture and often, I'm grateful to be able to report, to our amusement. Some of these stories were indeed funny as we look back on them, but were not so amusing at the moment. For example, there was the tale that we were German spies(!). We had come here during the war, the gossips pointed out. Henry's mother was born in Germany and spoke with a strong German accent—and so it was suspected that we had bought that house, way down there on the tip of the island, in order to signal enemy submarines.

Then there was the rumor that in our home we had a statue of Adolf Hitler(!). On our piano we had a statue of a British soldier, a garden ornament that had been made by a cousin of mine in Wales. The arms of the figure were so fastened that they could turn in the breeze to show the direction of the wind. Knowing that Mark and his young friends might damage this carved sailor if I fastened it to a fencepost outdoors, I kept it indoors. His upraised arm, it turns out, had suggested to some visitor a "Heil, Hitler!" salute. While we were greatly dismayed by such talk at the time, we can realize now how very much we were the subject of debate. We were, after all, the first family to move to the island in many years; and the peculiar timing of our arrival, in the midst of a terrible war, when people all over our country were unduly suspicious of "foreigners," also made us suspect.

Another tale that has amused us is the one about our immense wealth. It would seem that the simplicity in which we live, the frequent shabbiness of our clothes, and the knowledge of the tasks which our children do to assist in getting a college education should surely put the lie to that idea—yet it stubbornly persists.

"Oh, well," said Owen one day, "we have the prestige of wealth without the bother of looking after our money!"

We have gone a way on the road toward control of the tongue since living on Tangier Island. Unaware of the extent to which our most casual statement would be quoted and exaggerated, we were at first unfortunate in speaking our minds too freely, and sometimes too thoughtlessly. It is still a constant concern to keep our opinions in check where personalities are involved, and yet to be wise enough to speak fearlessly for the cause of the Christian way of life.

Indeed, there have been rough spots in the past years. They are at once forgotten, however, and sink into oblivion every time that Henry and I return to Tangier after an absence of even just a few days. The twenty-minute walk from the dock to Crab's Hole extends into an hour or more. First, we must stop at the electric plant to see if Junior Moore, the efficient young manager of the cooperative, has been getting along allright. All down the ridge we are met by those who we know by now are our true friends, who inquire about the children if we have been off visiting our youngsters, or who simply say, "I've missed you both going by!" We know they are sincere for they say the same to those who were born on the island. We know that they miss us as they would an old shoe, for they have now accepted us as part of the every-day life of Tangier. Sometimes we must stop on the way home to deliver articles we have bought in the city for various housewives. If our return has been anticipated we are often met with a plate of fried oysters or crabs, just to help out with our supper, and sometimes we are invited to Elizabeth Pruitt's for one of her good meals. Miss Nora or Miss Sadie will perhaps be standing by their fences to greet us, and Doris will run out to assure me as I pass that our pets whom she's been feeding during our absence are allright. As we cross the bridge over our deep canal the red siding and the white shutters of Crab's Hole come into view, while Maedchen and the cats run madly toward us, beside themselves with joy that we are back again. And together we philosophize as we drink the necessary cup of tea and look out over the marsh, peaceful in its late afternoon solitude. Always we conclude again and again that the people who have known us at our weakest as well as at our best are, in the long run, the closest of our friends.

And so, though we may yet wander far from this tiny island, we know that always we shall return to Tangier and to Crab's Hole. Too much mud has now adhered to our toes for us ever to be able to shake it off completely.

AFTERWORD

RICHARD HARWOOD

IN MID-MARCH 1994, I caught the noon mailboat from Crisfield to Tangier Island, a short hop of about twelve miles. The stern deck was loaded with soft drinks, lumber, steel rods, hardware, cement, and other goods essential to modern life on the island. Up front in the passenger compartment, women, speaking in a dialect forged on Tangier from Tidewater Virginian and Elizabethan English, gossiped and joked, glad to be headed home from the mainland where they had spent the night, waiting for the mailboat to arrive.

It was a chill, gusty day. The bay was choppy but the skies were clear. On such a day fifty years ago, Anne and Henry Jander made this trip to Tangier to a new life, a life recorded in *"Crab's Hole: A Family Story of Tangier Island."*

What had become of the Janders? What imprint did they leave on the island? Had they finally been accepted in this insular, clannish society of fewer than 1,000 people? Or were they remembered, if at all, as "outsiders" and unwelcome "meddlers" in a way of life that had persisted for generations? I thought I'd take a look and try to find out.

The Janders had too little time to get full answers to those questions. Henry Jander died from a heart attack while rushing to meet the mailboat in October 1951. Anne was then teaching a high school class at Tangier School. With Henry's death, she couldn't hang on, moved to New York, fell victim to rheumatoid arthritis but, indomitable as always, traveled to Europe to seek out distant relatives. She returned home and spent the last months of her life with her daughter, Sylvia. She died before Christmas in 1962 at the age of 57.

As the Janders had a half-century earlier, I found a friendly guide at the Tangier pier. He is John Bowden, a young waterman and jack-of-all-trades. He drove me on a golf cart through the neighborhoods and over to the southwest point of the island where the Janders had lived in isolation at Crab's Hole. The house, barns, and sheds were gone, along with the land on which they had stood.

"The bay took it," John Downey said. Nothing was left but a long, sweeping beach and unspoiled dunes covered with "water bushes" as sea grass is classed on Tangier. A few hundred yards offshore, the superstructures of a couple of World War II Liberty ships are visible. Navy airmen use them for target practice now and then.

This entire section of the island—the southwestern neck—is known as "Janders." The small wooden bridge leading to it across a canal is called "Jander's Bridge."

The family left other marks here. On the east coast of the island where the mail boat docks and watermen bring their catch, closely clustered houses and a few businesses dominate the waterfront. A memorial to the island's war veterans is on the main street. It carries the name of one of the Jander boys. A few hundred feet away, the power plant co-op, organized by Henry Jander to bring electricity to the island, now has generators that produce surplus power for sale to nearby Smith Island. Pictures of Henry and Anne Jander and newspaper clippings of their contributions to Tangier are mounted on the power plant walls. Anne is a slender dark-haired, serious-looking woman, wearing eyeglasses and an apron, a figure out of a Grant Wood painting. Henry is the picture of competence: a sturdy, compact man in steel-rimmed glasses, sleeves rolled up to the elbow.

Their ashes were planted in the little burial plot near Crab's Hole. Like the house and barns, the bay has taken the ashes, too. The bay brought the Janders to Tangier Island. The bay sustains the island's life. It is fitting it should claim the Janders. They took much from the bay and have given back themselves.

ANNE HUGHES JANDER spent a decade of her life as wife and mother to the Jander family when their home was on tiny Tangier Island, in the Chesapeake Bay. Choosing to leave urban pressures behind, the Janders moved to Tangier during World War II and remained there as the children grew and departed. Anne Jander began her memoir in 1943 and completed it in 1952. After her death ten years later, the then-adult children—Kent, Owen, Sylvia, and Mark—harbored it as an heirloom until they decided in the early 1990s to seek publication of their mother's remarkable story.

This book was set in Adobe Minion and Trajan
Composition & design by William C. Bowie

Cover design by Betsy Mitchell of Dolliver Church Design
Cover photographs hand-tinted by Alice Church Jones

Printed by BookCrafters, Fredericksburg, Virginia